MW00776356

Books by Nicole Keefer

STANDALONE

MY SAVIOR

Jimmy Yates Duology

His Victim's Torment (Book 1)

His Apprentice's Revenge (Book 2, Releasing August 2023)

Published by Flick-It-Books 2023

Second edition

ISBN: 978-1-959881-03-2 (ebook), 978-1-959881-04-09 (Paperback), 978-1-959881-05-06 (Hardback)

Library of Congress Cataloging-in-Publication data is available: 2022923010

Cover art by Booklytical Designs

Interior art by Nicole Nance

Editing by Glysia Gretz

For all the readers who fear monsters more than people, you have never seen the true evil of the world.

HIS VICTIM'S
TORMENT

NICOLE KEEFER

Prologue

This was already shaping up to be one hell of a case. Before even arriving at the scene, Metropolitan police detective Aaron Miller had a feeling this would be the case of the decade. He hoped he was wrong, and they weren't predestined to relive the horror that D.C. endured twenty-three years ago.

Detective Miller just pulled up to the crime scene when he saw one of the young officers run from the home and vomit in the rose bushes. It's not uncommon for officers to be sick at crime scenes, especially extremely violent ones like he was warned this one was.

No sooner had Detective Miller stepped out of his car, were cameras shoved in his face, blinding him with bright flashes. Even though he expected the scene to be crawling with the media, he still wanted to rip the camera out of every reporter's hands and smash them into tiny pieces.

He despised the media. People were just brutally murdered inside, and yes, the reporters were doing their jobs reporting the news, but they were vultures. They didn't care that the people lying dead inside were someone's loved ones. They just want to be the first ones to report on the grizzly scene.

"Officer, officer, is it true? Is this the work of Jimmy Yates? Is he back?" One reporter fired off questions faster than the detective could process.

How did the media hear about the details of this case before even he did? As soon as that question entered his mind, he knew the answer. Some media outlets enticed police officers by offering money for insider information. He unfortunately knew a few officers who lost their pensions for accepting deals with the media.

"The MPD has no comment at this time. Please excuse me." He pushed forward and started making his way into the house. If this was, in fact, the work of Jimmy Yates, he was dreading what he was walking into. He was a new officer when Yates terrorized the D.C. area in the 1990s. It was the black mark of his career that they never caught Yates before he seemed to drop off the map. Until today, Miller didn't think he'd ever have another chance to catch that bastard.

As soon as he walked into the house and saw the living room, he wanted to run outside and join the young officer in the rose bushes. No matter how many years he'd been a cop, nothing ever prepared him to walk into something like this. The sight before him was a page right out of a horror story. The story of Jimmy Yates. If this wasn't his work, it was an almost perfect copycat.

Thankfully, Yates was the only family annihilator that Miller has ever come across in his career. And now he was back, of that Miller was sure. If Yates followed the path he started in the early '90s, things in D.C. were going to get a lot worse, and fast. Yates never allowed much time to pass between murders.

Detective Miller took out his cell phone, knowing what he needed to do next. Damn it, he didn't want to do this. He wanted to be the one to catch this psychopath, but he knew he needed help. The safety of the citizens of his city came before his professional pride. "Dispatch, this is Detective Miller. Please connect me to the D.C. FBI field office."

Things are starting to progress nicely. He's been away long enough that the ignorant law enforcement agents that have been trying to track him down for years have become lazy and complacent. He stood in the back of the crowd, watching everyone run around like chickens with their heads cut off. Smiling, he couldn't help thinking, 'wouldn't that be a sight to see?'

A surge of euphoria came over him when a young officer rushed out of the house and lost his breakfast. He couldn't suppress his laugh. He loved that his work could still shock and awe people. What he did to those sinners was a work of art. People should marvel at his labor. This was just the opening scene, and the fun was yet to come. Returning to D.C. was never something he thought about doing until he saw her photo in the paper. There she was, smiling up at the Dean of George-town University, and it sent him into a rage. No bitch had ever caused him so many issues. Why couldn't she have died like a good little girl?

After he killed her parents, they hid her away behind a wall of secu-rity. Not any longer, though. Now she's finally back within reach, and this time she wouldn't get away. He'd been watching her for about two weeks now. Finding out where she lived was easy. All he had to do was get buddy-buddy with one of her students. Knowing her class schedule allowed him time to install cameras around her apartment complex and the school, making it easy to keep track of her. Like hell he would lose her again.

He needed this kill to put his world back in order. Needing to be closer to the action, he wove his way through the throngs of people, moving closer to the police tape that blocked the way to his master-piece. Surely no one would recognize him. It'd been over twenty years since he graced D.C. with his presence. An eager young officer came charging up to the cop guarding the driveway and announced that the FBI were on their way. Yes, things were progressing nicely, according to his plans.

Now, to put the rest into play. He should've made this kill quick and then moved back out of D.C. but she'd been a tormenting presence in his life for so long. Wanting her and her family to suffer before the end was his only goal. They all needed to know that he was coming and there was nothing that would stop him from killing her. This was the endgame. Now let the fun begin.

Chapter 1

The phone call that could make the unit chief of the D.C. FBI field offices career came in ten minutes ago, and Chief Parker knew, if he closed this case, he'd be on the fast track to promotion. Knowing he couldn't run the complete investigation himself, as much as he wanted to, he'd need to pull his best agent. Unfortunately, his best agent was an arrogant son of a bitch that was hard to control. This one time, it didn't matter; he needed the best. Picking up the phone, he told his secretary to get Agent Walker to his office now.

As soon as he walked into the office for the day, the chief had already summoned him to his office. He was, however, still in complete shock over the information he received once he was there. The FBI had been after this serial killer since Walker was a little boy. He studied his criminal activity in college, then again at Quantico. It would be the opportunity of a lifetime to be the one to put him behind bars.

As soon as Agent Devon Walker stepped out of the unit chief's office, his partner, Agent Michael Matthews, ran up and stopped him. "Hey Walker, so are the rumors true? Is Yates back? Are we on the case?" His partner was moving so swiftly, Walker had to put an arm out to steady him so he didn't knock them both over.

1

"That's what it looks like. Chief Parker said the mayor is going bal-listic and wants all hands on deck. There haven't been any other killings in D.C. in decades with the same MO as Jimmy Yates. He's one sick bastard. We need to jump on this quickly and get ahead of him before he butchers another family." Walker felt sick to his stomach, remember-ing the photos the chief had shown him of the latest crime scene. What kind of person could do something like that to another human being, let alone a family? By God, what he did to the children was diabolical. Never in all his years as an agent had he seen something as horrific, and he'd seen some pretty sadistic crap. "Chief Parker said that we needed to check someone out. A survivor, the only survivor. Apparently, Yates screwed up back in 1995 and left a five-year-old girl alive. Parker thinks Yates will try to finish what he started twenty-three years ago. He wants her notified right away and placed in the care of the FBI. He's hoping Yates will get sloppy and we can catch him if he goes for her."

Agent Matthews walked over to his computer and started typing like a maniac. Matthews was a wiz with the research aspect of a case, and Walker was a master at taking a suspect down and getting them to talk.That's why they were such a good team. Matthews was spouting off questions as he typed, not once looking up from his computer screen as Walker gave him the information he needed. "Was it ever determined how she survived? Yates always made sure there were no survivors. It's not in his MO to miss someone. I would have assumed he would go back and finish what he started right after he failed the first time. He's an annihilator killer. Doctors and scientists analyzed every aspect of these cases and determined that Yates did some long-term, very in-depth surveillance. He had to have been watching them for a while because he made sure all members of the family were home so he could wipe them out in a single shot."

Walker shook his head. "At the time, the detectives tried to get the story from the girl, but of course, it traumatized her. The state stopped the questioning when her aunt and uncle came from Pennsylvania to get her. It seems her uncle is an important political figure in Pennsylvania. He showed up with a bunch of lawyers and swept her away. They kept the documents sealed in hopes of hiding her location from Yates. Poor little girl. She was home while it happened. I can't imagine being in the house while my family is being murdered. It must have been a hundred times worse for a five-year-old. It's a wonder she survived, let alone that she didn't end up in a psychiatric hospital. And damn if she didn't make something of herself."

Agent Matthews handed Walker a paper with the information they needed to contact the witness. Mary Anderson, age 28. Doctor of Forensic Psychology. Professor at Georgetown University right here in D.C. Unmarried, no children, and no criminal record. Not even a parking ticket. From the teaching evaluations Matthews found, students and staff loved Ms. Anderson. Her classes were in such high demand that there's a waiting list.

Walker scanned the information. "At least it looks like she was able to pull herself together after the trauma she experienced. We see a lot of children in these situations that end up on the wrong side of the law, and all because of something that happened to them that was beyond their control."

Walker went to his desk and gathered his weapon and credentials. "Come on Matthews, let's take a ride. If we jump on this now, we could be back before lunch."

Most people were already at work by this time of the morning, so the D.C. traffic had thankfully tapered off. Walker and Matthews made it to Georgetown University in record time and it only took a few minutes to get directions to the psychology building where Ms. Anderson was teaching. The building was easy to navigate, so they made it to her class, with some time remaining, before the students were released. Instead of interrupting her teaching, they waited in the back of the lecture hall and observed.

The lecture hall's lights were out for the presentation being conducted, and it took a moment for their eyes to adjust. Ms. Anderson was at the front of the dimmed auditorium, and by the looks of her slide show, was giving a lecture on John Wayne Gacy. The slide, taking up much of the wall directly behind her, was of Gacy dressed in his iconic Patches the Clown costume. Glancing around the auditorium, Walker noticed the students hanging on their professor's every word.

This certainly wasn't like any college class he remembers taking. All of his college classes were boring courses with boring professors that made him fall asleep. He suffered through those classes because, in order to become an FBI agent, he needed a college degree. After much thought, he decided on a degree in criminal justice, since it coincided with his career goal. And one thing was for damn sure, none of his professors looked like her. He may not have slept through so many lectures if they did. She continued for another fifteen minutes before her teacher's assistant turned the lights back on.

Ms. Anderson glanced in their direction. She was aware they were intruding on her class, but didn't stop teaching. Ms. Anderson turned out to be the total opposite of what Walker pictured. Matthews had pulled up photos online from various charity functions and university outings, but the presence she emitted in person was dynamic. Even from the back of the room, he could see that her eyes were sapphire blue and enchanting. They shined especially bright against her tan face. Mary wore simple jeans, a white blouse, and a midnight blue blazer. Though she wasn't very tall, she possessed a sort of tough elegance. She was the type of woman that caught people's attention. She was the type of woman that people liked to watch.

He wondered how many of these young students took the class for the content or took it to watch her. He'd bet at least a handful of the students had a crush on Ms. Anderson. She was an incredibly beautiful woman. But did her personality match? He hadn't met many children of politicians that were even half civil. She was the niece of a powerful politician, but she was close enough to be his daughter since he raised her from the time parents died.

She was winding down and handing out a heavy homework assignment. He couldn't help but smile over the groans from a few of the students. "Now remember, midterms are due Friday. No exceptions. That means you, Georgie. I will not accept any 'the dog ate my midterm excuses.' This is college, for goodness' sakes. Do the damn assignment." The student sighed loud enough for the professor to hear him, and she smiled.

"Yes, Ms. A," multiple students called out, including Georgie.

As soon as the last student funneled out of the hall, the two agents made their way down to the podium, where Ms. Anderson was packing up her belongings and speaking to her teacher's assistant. The young man looked up at the two agents coming down the aisle, said something to Ms. Anderson, then turned and walked away.

Walker flashed his badge with his left hand while reaching out with his right hand. "Ms. Anderson, I'm Agent Devon Walker. I'm with the FBI, and this is my partner, Agent Matthews. Do you have someplace private where we can talk for a moment?" Her back went rigid. "Yes, of course. Let me just grab a few things, then we can head over to my office. I have a few hours until my next class. I was just going to grade some papers."

She took a moment to gather her belongings. Carefully stacking papers and folders, then placing them into a very fancy, very expensive-looking briefcase with her initials engraved on a gold plate on the front. Walker knew a Jack George briefcase when he saw one. It was the same brand his father carried, and very similar to the one his father gave him when he graduated from the FBI academy. It was a very extravagant accessory compared to her apparel. Devon wondered if hers had sentimental meaning, or if she just liked pretty things.

She led them out of the classroom and into her office, right across the hall. She motioned for them to take a seat, then turned and shut the door. Without asking, she went to the mini-fridge on a small table on the back wall, reached in, pulled out three water bottles, and handed them to each of the agents. Once she was back at her desk and seated, she addressed the agents.

"Now, what can I do for you, agents? It's not every day we have the FBI on campus." She started wringing her hands, dreading the information she anticipated was coming. If something happened to her aunt or uncle, their personal security would've come and told her, so that only left one thing. The one thing that haunted her since she was a little girl. The one thing she knew would catch up to her one day.

Walker was straight to the point. No need to sugarcoat things. "Miss, we have reason to believe Jimmy Yates is back in D.C."

To his relief, she didn't panic or break down crying, even though he saw her demeanor drastically change. He noticed how she instinctively reached for a ring on her left ring finger. It was delicate, silver, and with a small emerald. It must have meant a great deal to her. From the research Matthews performed this morning, he knew Ms. Anderson wasn't married, so the ring must have other special significance. He also noticed that she blanched at the mention of Jimmy Yates, but kept her composure. Strong woman.

"Yates? Back in D.C.? Are you sure? No one has heard from him in years. My uncle's even had people looking for him since that psycho killed my parents. My mother was my uncle's sister."

Agent Matthews addressed her next. "Yes, miss, we're sure it's him. The MPD notified us this morning that they have a current case that follows Yates's MO to the smallest detail."

She shook, her eyes turned bright with unshed tears, and held back the bile that she could taste in her mouth. "So, there is no one left? That's correct, right? He killed the entire family, even the children?"

"Yes, miss," Matthews answered.

Her jaw tightened and lips pursed at the way they addressed her as miss. It was clear it agitated her, and Walker wondered how long it would take for her to speak up, but he wasn't going to say anything. He enjoyed watching the emotions play across her face, and he didn't need to wait long for a reaction.

"We won't let anything happen to you, miss. We–"

"Please," she interrupted, louder than she intended. "Will you please stop calling me 'miss'? Will you please call me Mary?" She asked assertively, but quietly.

Matthews looked at Walker like he wanted his approval. Walker couldn't help but smile and nodded slightly. It was FBI policy to address a person professionally and not too informally, especially with potential witnesses or victims. Matthews was a by-the-books agent and didn't adjust to change very well. That's another reason they were such great partners. Walker would throw the book out the window if he'd be able to get away with it, and Matthews reminded him he wouldn't look good in orange. They balance each other out.

"Mary," Walker started, "the FBI would like to offer you a security detail until we're able to apprehend Jimmy Yates. Somebody would be with you twenty-four hours a day. We'll keep you safe."

"Why? Why me? And why now? Do you really think I have something to worry about? Of course you do, or you wouldn't be here. But surely Yates would've forgotten about me. It's been so many years. He hasn't tried to contact me since the night he murdered my parents. I mean, really, it's been over twenty years." With every statement, Mary fought back the tears threatening to spill down her cheeks.

"Mary, do you really think Yates would have forgotten about you? You're a Doctor of Forensic Psychology. You make a living analyzing serial killers and figuring out what makes them tick. I would bet you went into this field because of what happened to you as a child. If you take a moment to think about it, you know Yates destroys entire families. Everyone. So, it's safe to assume Yates would consider you a failure, a mark against him. You're the one that got away. And that's not something he'd accept. We don't feel it's a coincidence he's back in D.C."

She reached her right hand up and rubbed her face, then rubbed back into her hair. "Of course, Yates is the reason I chose the field I'm in. I wanted to understand what made that psychopath murder not only my whole family but many other entire families, too. He destroyed my life when he took my parents from me. The only reason I'm alive is because he couldn't find me. Not for lack of trying, though. He practically ripped that house apart until he heard someone at the front door. Thank goodness for the mailman's incompetence, and my neighbors' greed. If it wasn't for them, I have no doubt he would have eventually found me."

This piqued Walker's interest. Nothing he read explained how she survived that night. "Can you please explain to me what you meant by him not being able to find you? Your case file was a bit sparse in detail. They sealed some parts of your file right after the court order your uncle filed, and even the FBI cannot view them. Any information you can provide to us about that night may be invaluable in apprehending him."

"Certainly, anything to help you catch this creep." Mary took a deep breath. She was about to relive what her aunt and uncle had spent so much time and money trying to help her forget. But if it would help get Yates off the street and behind bars, she would relive it a thousand times more. Her parents deserved to have their murderer caught, and she wouldn't put her terror above justice for them. They would want her to be strong.

"As you know, Yates takes out entire families. I concluded later that he watched us for an extended amount of time to know our routine. It's the only feasible explanation how he knew when to strike. On that terrible night, it was about six p.m.; I know this because we just finished

9

dinner. Mom was fanatical about dinner being at five-fifteen sharp every night that we didn't have other activities scheduled. Even though I was so young, I still remember that. It must be something my grandparents did because my uncle also likes dinner at five fifteen on the dot. After dinner, I went into what my father called my play place and I would normally stay there until it was time to get ready for bed."

"Could you please elaborate on this play place? Was this place somewhere outside? Is that how you were able to elude Yates?" Agent Walker asked, while Agent Matthews took notes.

Mary shook her head. "Our house was quite small, and my father wanted me to have a safe place to play without giving up the office or being outside where they couldn't keep an eye on me. So, he built me one inside the house. A place that was just mine, where I could do and be anything I wanted. It was a child's dream. Underneath our staircase was completely open, so my father framed it out and made it my own area. He even painted it pink with pictures of butterflies. My mother didn't want a normal doorknob because she thought it would look out of place, so my father made the opening a panel that you would push to open. But the panel could also lock from the inside and thank God it could. When it locked, the panel wouldn't budge at all when touched. If you didn't know the door was there, you wouldn't even know there was a space under the stairs. It looked just like a wall. It saved my life." Her voice broke with emotion.

Agent Walker paused and gave her a moment to gather her thoughts. When she nodded she was ready to continue, he softly said, "Go on."

After internally composing herself, and embracing the subtle encouragement from the agent, Mary took one last deep, shaking breath, then continued. "Yates knew I was home. He had to have known we were all home, or else he wouldn't have attacked that night. After he bound my parents, he turned his attention to looking for me. Right after I heard Yates call out for me, my father screamed for me to stay where I was. As a little kid, I wanted to rush out of the room and help my parents, but there was something in my father's voice that made me stay put. I never heard my father sound like that, and it terrified me. There was such desperation in his voice.

"After my parents stopped screaming, I heard this unfamiliar voice calling out to me. The more he called my name, the more frustrated he seemed to get. I could hear him throwing our stuff around the house, turning over beds, pulling things out of closets, all to find me. It sounded like he was tearing our house apart wall by wall. I'll never forget his taunts. He went around the house yelling, 'come out, come out, wherever you are'. Or 'Marco'. Did he really expect me to answer back? I remember being terrified. But because my father was an amazing carpenter, he never even knew how close he was to me the whole time. I heard him walk past me at least five times. Each time, I thought he would finally find me. I would hold my breath when he came close, thinking he'd be able to hear my heart pounding."

"You mentioned the mailman. How did he play into having Yates leave the house?" Agent Matthews asked curiously.

"Our mailman was always mixing up our address with our neighbors. That's what happened that day. Mr. Smith, our neighbor, came over to deliver a package. He rang the doorbell for a long time. He did this because any time he brought us one of our packages, mom would always give him some baked goods for helping us out. Sometimes I thought he had an understanding with the mailman to purposely mix up

11

the packages so he could get some cookies. I've never seen a grown man have such a sweet tooth. I used to announce that the cookie monster was at the door, but my dad didn't like me saying that. He said it wasn't lady-like to make fun of other people and I might hurt Mr. Smith's feelings. Secretly, I think daddy thought the nickname was funny."

She smirked a bit. "So, if it wasn't for the neighbor wanting his reward for returning our mail, Yates may have eventually found me. I waited what seemed like forever after Yates left and the neighbor stopped ringing the doorbell to come out from under the stairs. I remember running to the phone in the kitchen to call 911. And then I went to find my parents. I'm not sure what happened after that. The next thing I remember, I woke up in the hospital and my aunt and uncle were there. I knew something terrible had happened because I had only ever seen them on special occasions. They told me very few details about that night, but they had to tell me my parents were dead and I was going to come live with them. Things have come back in bits and pieces since then, but there's much I still don't remember." The nightmares and memories bombarded her. Waves of despair washed over her. She shuddered from the pain. It's over. She needed to forget it. Her mind wasn't listening as she tried telling herself this over and over. She absently reached for her ring again and took several deep breaths.

It was surprising how much she remembered. From the file he read, she was in an almost catatonic state when the FBI tried to question her. He noticed a sudden change in her demeanor. She was shaking and became pale. It was a normal reaction for anyone who'd survived such a horrific event. "Mary, are you okay?" Obviously, she wasn't okay, and he meant to distract her with questions.

"Fine. I'm fine. You'd think a person who makes dissecting the minds of serial killers her life's work wouldn't break down when talking about one. I'm just being ridiculous. Sorry."

"That may be true, Mary, but not every doctor in your profession had their lives personally turned upside down by the very thing they study. You have every reason to break down occasionally."

She reached over, gently took his hand, and smiled at him. "Thank you, Agent Walker."

What was wrong with him? He felt his muscles tighten at her touch, and he was sure she heard his breath hitch in his throat. His heart raced, and his temperature rose. It was like a jolt of electricity fired into his arm. Eyes darting to her face, he couldn't help but feel lost in her ravishing sapphire blue eyes. He'd never felt like this when any other woman touched him. He had to get it together. This wasn't professional. This was a witness, not some floozy from a bar he picked up. Pulling his hand back, he decided he needed to change the subject, fast. "Now, Mary, we'd like to place you into protective custody with an FBI agent. We'd prefer you take time away from your classes and let us move you to a safe house until we catch Yates. We need to have you secure 24/7. The easiest way to do that is to keep you in a single location. We would allow you to inform your aunt and uncle of your location, but no other friends or colleagues."

He already knew what the answer was as soon as she started shaking her head. "No. Absolutely not. That monster took too much away from me already for me to give up more because of him. I'm not going to stop living my life because he may or may not decide to seek me out again. I'm training the next generation of forensic psychologists. This work is too important to place on hold. These students deserve my undivided attention. They could be the ones to help catch people like Yates in the future, and I'll not give that up. I'll also not be holed up in some run-down motel in the middle of God knows where until you people can apprehend him. Look, he's gotten away from the FBI so many times before, and if he does it again, I won't be forced out of the life I made for myself just so the bureau can save face if Yates finishes the job and finally kills me. I'm sick of living in fear. I'm done running. If I agree to any security, it'll be on my terms, and I get to stay in my home and continue my classes. My uncle made sure my apartment was secure when I moved in. If you're so set on protecting me, protect me, but I'm not stopping my life for him."

Walker knew just by looking at her, she was going to be trouble. He pitied whatever poor agent would get the assignment. They'd have their hands full trying to keep Ms. Anderson in line.

Chapter 2

After making it back to the FBI building, they weren't even two steps off the elevator, and all eyes were on them. Or, more accurately, they were on Mary Anderson. Most of the other agents were staring at her with fascination as being *the one that got away*. Devon couldn't blame them. All agents learned about Jimmy Yates at the academy, and she was a main part of his story. The agents that were looking at her with disgusting grins, need to fix their professionalism straight away.

With her eyes on her feet, Mary didn't notice all the glances. They walked down a short hallway before stopping at an ugly brown door. Interrogation? No, that should be in the back of the building. Devon moved in front of her and held the door open.

"I need you to wait in here while I go check in with my boss. You'll be more comfortable here than out in the main lobby." Pointing to the cabinets and fridge, "there are plenty of snacks and things to drink. Hopefully, someone will be along shortly."

Without giving her time to thank him for his consideration, Devon turned and walked out the door. Leaving her with nothing but her thoughts.

He didn't even make it back to his desk when Chief Parker called him and Matthews into his office. "You two just got back from visiting Ms. Anderson, correct? Do you have her secure? Where is she? She needs to get all packed up and out of D.C. as soon as possible."

Both agents nodded, but Walker answered. "Yes, Chief. We have her. She's in the conference room waiting to be escorted home. I told her it shouldn't be too long until you can assign someone for her protection. She has an ultimatum, though. Mary's determined not to have her life interrupted in any way. She's refusing to leave D.C. but will accept protection. Whoever you assign to her will have their hands full."

Chief Parker didn't speak for a few minutes as he paced behind his desk, and that worried Walker. He didn't know what was going on inside Parker's head, but he knew it couldn't be good. "Ok, Agent Walker. Since Ms. Anderson refuses to leave D.C., she is now your responsibility. As of right now, I officially reassigned you to protection duty. You're going to stick to Ms. Anderson like glue. You don't let her out of your sight. Anywhere she goes, you go. Day and night, night and day."

There was no way Walker was going to be on babysitting duty. He was a senior field agent, for goodness' sakes, not a fresh recruit out of the academy. "But Chief, why me? I'm not a newbie. And I sure as shit am not a babysitter. I'd be of better use working this case and catching this psycho. For real, what's my next assignment?" Walker had much better things he could do with his time besides watching a woman who, on the off chance, could become a target again. Especially a woman who seemed hell-bent on continuing her life like normal and making the person protecting her life completely miserable. It'd be different if she'd stay where they put her, but she made that clear that wasn't going to happen. The job was better suited for one of the younger agents. He also knew it would be best to distance himself from her, at least until he understood the reaction he had to her in her office.

The chief knew he was going to have a fight with Agent Walker. Yes, he was one of his best agents, and that's exactly the reason he was assigning him to watch Ms. Anderson. He couldn't trust this with just any agent. He needed one he knew would put his life on the line to see the job complete, and that was Walker. All eyes were going to be on this case, and he didn't need the brass breathing down his neck if some newbie screwed up. Walker's service record was exemplary, and that's why Parker chose him above all others. "You have no idea who that young lady is, do you, Walker?"

Walker shrugged. He wasn't in the mood to play guessing games. Walker got along with the chief fine, but he suspected he had a personal agenda that didn't always coincide with the best intentions for the Bureau. "Of course I do. She's Yates's only surviving victim."

The chief waved his hand. "Yes, yes. Of course, she is that. But... She is the niece of Congressman Robert Carter of Pennsylvania. The very influential, very aggressive, Congressman from Pennsylvania. He's a powerful man in congress, and someone you don't want to be on the bad side of. I've seen careers ruined because they crossed someone in congress and damn it, that won't happen to me. I don't know why I never put the two together until the director called and told me her safety is top priority. He doesn't need someone on the Hill making waves. And Congressman Carter has friends in very high places, like White House places, so I won't have his niece's protection botched by some inexperienced agent. Do you get that? You stick to her like glue. I mean it."

Walker wanted to snap off the finger the chief was pointing in his face. "Her uncle has an entire security force at his disposal. Why can't he provide his own protection for her? Let him be responsible for her. She's his family, after all."

Parker slammed his open palm onto his desk and sent a sharp sound reverberating through the room. "Stop whining, Agent Walker. It's unbecoming of you. It's already decided. And that's an order. You already told her yourself that the FBI wants to provide a protection detail, and that detail is going to be you, so deal with it. Her family will definitely hire their own security, but we'll have one of our own on the inside. Just keep her alive while we catch Yates." Chief Parker dismissed the two agents when his phone rang. It was the director, again. This was going to be a hell of a case. The director would want results, fast, and wouldn't allow any room for excuses.

As soon as they were out of the chief's office, Matthews burst out laughing. Walker turned to him and gave him a glare that would've intimidated anyone else, but they were partners, and he knew he wouldn't stay mad at him. For Matthews, Walker was all bluster and no action.

Matthews saw the way his partner looked at Mary. She intrigued him, and he could see Walker would try to dissect everything about her until he understood exactly what made her tick. This was going to be interesting. He wished he could be a fly on the wall in her apartment. He bet the fireworks would set off in no time. Now, would the fireworks be Mary setting Walker on fire, or fireworks of intimacy? He would sit back with the popcorn and enjoy the show as he watched to find out which it would be.

Walker knew there was no getting out of this detail. He's never known the chief to change his mind on a decision after making it. He'd need to make the best of it. Do his job and keep his distance. He was an FBI agent. She had to listen to him. He's the law.

Mary was exasperated, sitting in an FBI headquarters' conference room with boring decor, nothing to do, and no word on when she'd be able to go home. They took her phone when she entered the FBI building, and she just wanted to call her uncle and warn him about what was going on, but without her phone, she had to sit there and do nothing. After the day she had, the stark white walls seemed to close in on her. She wanted to go home and have a very large glass of wine, jump into a nice hot bath, and forget today ever happened. Not that it was in any way possible that she'd be able to forget Yates was back and she was possibly a target yet again. Wasn't it bad enough that he took almost everything away from her?

If it wasn't for her aunt and uncle, she'd have been in the foster system and no clue where she'd be in life. She had little confidence in the justice system when it came to Yates. He'd been on the loose for over twenty years since her parents' murder. But he was murdering long before that and they still hadn't apprehended him. And who knows how many other families he'd killed in that time? It turned her stomach to think about it. Now she was going to have her privacy disrupted by some FBI agent who would try to control her life. Nope. That wouldn't happen.

Just then, the door glided open and Agent Walker sauntered in, case file flimsily waving in his hand. In an unreasonable reaction, her pulse raced. She shifted backwards in her chair, trying hard not to let him see her struggling to keep her composure. They just parted company, and she resolved herself to hoping it would be a very long time before she saw him again. At this time in her life, there was no room for relationships. But from the first time she laid eyes on the black-haired knockout, all she thought about was tearing his shirt off and taking him back to her apartment. Those thoughts would only bring trouble, and also inappropriate because of the circumstance in which they even met.

He sauntered over to where she was sitting on the opposite side of the room and sat down next to her. Looking straight into her eyes, she held her breath. "Mary, since you have decided, against the judgment of the FBI, to refuse offsite protective custody in a place of twenty-four seven security, my superior decided I will be the agent in charge of your safety until we apprehend Jimmy Yates." He held up his hand when she opened her mouth to protest. "What this means is that from this moment on, I will not be leaving your side. We will be so close by the time Yates is behind bars that I'll know all your little secrets." That last sentence he said with a mischievous grin.

Crap. Of course, they had assigned him as her protection detail. Why couldn't they give her someone less attractive? Someone that didn't send shivers down her body with every smile. Mary was even more rattled. She knew the intent of the FBI was to give her protection to keep her safe. She was used to security being around, with her uncle being a congressman, but she didn't want every moment of her life analyzed. And to top it all off, they assign someone to her with eyes so green she could feel herself drowning in them if she stared too long. Ugh. Agent Walker was going to be a distraction that she really didn't need. She also felt he wouldn't be easy to manipulate to allow her the liberties that some of her uncle's security officers have done in the past. There were a few times when she was younger that she'd be able to get the security guys to let her bend the rules just by giving them a little smile. It's doubtful a smile would work on this agent. Damn it.

Walker was enjoying watching the play of emotions crossing Mary's face. "You don't look very happy with my chief's decision. Honestly, I'm not looking forward to this either, but I'm here to stay, like it or not. I'm going to try to give you as much space as I can in the time that we are together. Sometimes, that won't be possible, but I'll try. You just need to understand right now that your safety comes first, before your feelings or your privacy. I'm making a guess here, but you won't agree to go away for a few weeks, would you? I can get the FBI to splurge for maybe a little island retreat until we caught Yates. You could relax on the beach and drink some Mai Tais."

She shook her head, confirming the refusal he already expected. Why was this woman so difficult? Mostly anyone would jump at the opportunity for an all-expenses paid island vacation on the government's dime. But in the short hours he'd known Ms. Anderson, he already concluded she was nothing like anyone he'd ever met. He just hasn't decided yet if it was a good thing, or a bad thing.

"Right now is really not a good time to leave on a vacation. I'm in the middle of a semester. These kids paid for their class, and there's a waiting list to get into the classes I teach. I won't let them down by having my TA, Markus, teach the rest of the term while I fly off to who knows where, even though he is more than capable. You'll need to understand that right now. I won't turn my life upside down over the remote possibility this bastard is going to come after me again. You haven't given me proof I'm a target."

He shook his head. So it begins, she was being contrary. "For now, as long as I can keep you safe, we'll work something out so you're still able to teach. I'll work with the university to verify the kids in your class are who they say they are. Everyone will have a background check. We will check all students and teachers that may come in contact with you. If anything looks out of place, you won't be stepping foot on that campus. Keeping you alive is more important than a semester of classes and your student's feelings. If you work with me, I'll try to work with you. Got it?"

"Got it. But it's not my kids you need to watch for. It's Yates. And I can tell you with a one hundred percent guarantee Yates is not a student in any of my classes. That, I think I would have noticed."

"I'm not leaving anything to chance. Most people would do anything for the right amount of money. If Yates knew he couldn't get to you, he could pay someone to draw you out. Think of this scenario: Yates comes up to one of your students pretending to be an ex-lover trying to reconnect with you. The story may pull at their heartstrings and they could tell him the schedule of your every move, on and off campus. When you'll be alone, when you'll be traveling, and maybe even your home address if they know it. Nothing, and I mean nothing, gets overlooked, and that includes your students. Now, let's get out of here and we can nail down your schedule later. Is there anywhere you need to go? My Chief said it would be okay for us to hold up at your apartment instead of an FBI safe house location. He wants you to be as comfortable as possible since we're not sure how long you'll need the protection detail. We're assuming your security is already top notch, considering your uncle and aunt would want to make sure you are protected. We'll just build off their already in-place protections. The FBI will go over everything and make sure the building is secure and watched at all times."

She looked at her watch and realized she only had about an hour until her next class. "We need to head back to Georgetown. My next class starts at three. Is that okay?" If he agreed, they'd be cutting it close with getting back to campus in the afternoon traffic.

Agent Walker thought about it for a moment. They hadn't yet checked out any of the students. "It should be too soon for Yates to have a coordinated strategy. So, you can go to this one class, but after this, no more until we can perform our checks, and I get the all clear. I'll look around the school, but until I can coordinate with campus security, if I don't feel you are safe, we are leaving. Agreed?"

The feeling was back again. The frustration about having her life micromanaged. "We'll see." She turned and walked out the door, back down the hall, to the elevator that would take them to the parking garage. She instinctively reached down to touch her ring, taking a deep breath.

Mary didn't even realize they'd arrived back at campus until Agent Walker asked her where it would be convenient for him to park. It wasn't often that she became so lost in thought that minutes passed–or in this case around thirty minutes–with her spacing in her head that recognition of the outside world was forgotten.

After some guidance, Walker parked next to the psychology building and told her to stay in the car until he came around. He opened the door for her and took hold of her arm as they crossed the street. The wind caught them and the scent of her perfume, one he recognized as Givenchy Rose Ardente, lifted from her unbound hair. It smelled better on her than on his ex-girlfriend.

As soon as they were in the building, she turned to face him, noticing his eyes were looking everywhere but at her. "Agent Walker, was that really necessary? I can walk by myself. I'm a big girl. You're treating me like a child that needs guidance. People will notice and they will talk. I don't care about gossip, but I don't want any questions. When this is all over, I'll still need to work here. There is going to be enough gossip when this all hits the news, and my past gets dredged up again."

"First off, yes, it was necessary. Get used to it. You don't open any more car doors; I will do that for you. You don't go first into any room or building. When we enter a room, you stay by the door until I'm able to verify no one's lurking in any dark corners waiting to strike. Just get used to me being in front of you, behind you, or beside you for the foreseeable future. You're stuck with me until we find Yates. It won't help you to argue. That's just the way it's going to be."

Instantly, her head was pounding. She was so overwhelmed and confused. "Why can't I open any more doors? That seems very excessive to me."

Walker let out a sigh. He really didn't want to explain this to her, but maybe if she took this threat a little more seriously, it would make his job easier. "The reason you can't open any more doors is that you are not trained to look for explosive triggers. I am. Any more questions?"

Shock pulsed through her. "What did you say? What do you mean, explosive triggers?"

He looked her up and down, noticing the confusion on her face. "Exactly what I said. An explosive that is placed in or under a vehicle or door is a very effective way to injure or kill an unexpecting victim. I'm trained to spot them, and you're not. Therefore, I go first. Always."

Man, it was going to be a long afternoon. "Fine." She turned and started towards her office. She reached for the doorknob when he knocked her hand away.

"You don't listen very well, do you? I just got done telling you: I go into rooms first, and I open the doors, not you. Remember that. I'm here to protect you, so let me do my job. Don't make this hard on yourself. If you can't obey my rules, I'll get the FBI to ship you to some hole in the wall town in Wyoming. And they'll do it regardless if you like it or not. They're the federal government."

His threats seemed to hit home. He saw her eyes blazing, which is what he wanted. He didn't want to threaten her, but she didn't seem to understand the severity of her situation. It was better for her to be scared than to treat this nonchalantly. Complacency is deadly.

She finally decided arguing with him would do no good. "Fine. After you," she said sarcastically. They walked into her office and he made a quick glance around. There was no place for anyone to hide. "There, are you satisfied? Can I please get to work now? I have phone calls to return and emails to check."

Noticing she looked forlorn, he said, "Buck up. It could be worse."

"How?" She couldn't believe for one moment that it could get any worse than having all her privacy taken away from her.

"Well, you could have Agent Scott as your bodyguard. He hits on anything with two legs and a skirt."

She couldn't tell if he was joking or not, but he had a big grin on his face. And boy, did he look good when he smiled. How could she go from one minute being so frustrated at him to the next, thinking about how damn good he looked? Finally realizing what she was doing, she pulled her gaze from his mouth. Ugh. What was wrong with her? She knew what was wrong. Her emotions were all over the place since find-ing out she may be a target for Yates again. That guy was sadistic, so she had every right to be flustered. Who wouldn't be upset about being a target for a serial killer?

Walker continued. "And while we're at it, we're going to be chummy for a while, so why not drop the formalities and you call me by my first name, Devon? While you're here on campus and in class, I'll try to blend in so your students don't get freaked out or curious about an FBI agent watching their teacher. I'll even attempt to keep my weapon concealed. Although it's always fun to see who gets nervous around law enforcement, it's a good indicator they have something to hide. But in retrospect, that might make my job harder, so I'll try to be inconspicu-ous. Deal?"

"Deal." She let out a sigh of relief. Until that moment, she didn't even consider how her students would react to a stranger in their class, let alone an FBI agent. Most of her students knew about her past. One even admitted that's what drew him to register for the course. But there was no reason to scare her students or have them think their safety was at risk. She would be open with them and explain the situation only if the need arose.

Without being asked to, Devon was kind enough to step out of the room when she had to return a call to the Dean of the University to ex-plain the situation about Devon and the FBI. Devon's chief had called the Dean, but he wanted to get more information straight from Mary, and make sure she was okay. He was protective of his students to a fault, and Mary was sure she'd need to calm him down with the upheaval that came from close surveillance, background checks, and an FBI presence on his campus. Meanwhile, Devon took his time watching students funneling into the lecture hall to get ready for class. He didn't like the idea of Mary being here before he could run background checks on her students, but he would adjust. Always being on guard was part of the job.

As soon as Mary touched the doorknob, Devon was ready to escort her to class. He didn't lecture her again about the door, but he gave her the look instead. She'd only known him a few hours, but it was his 'you really don't listen to me' look. It was the same one she'd received multiple times since leaving the bureau office. And she had a feeling she'd be on the receiving end of a lot more of those looks. She really had a problem taking orders, and an issue with not getting her way. She was the only one who knew what was best for her, and she wasn't about to take a stranger's criticism when it came to her well-being. "What should I tell my students as to why there is a stranger with me? I have a rule, the only people allowed in the lecture hall are the ones who registered for the class. No one else, no exceptions. They know I don't break my rules for any reason, so they'll become suspicious and are bound to ask questions."

He shrugged. "Tell them whatever you want. Tell them I'm another professor if that helps." He got a big smile on his face again. "You can tell them I'm your boyfriend. Maybe that'll stop the questions. Or I could just flash my badge and gun, but I figured you still want me to be low key."

She laughed. "How about we stick with the professor? You're way out of my league anyway, and those students would know it. The students I've had in multiple classes over the last few years don't have any reservation about giving me advice on my non-existent love life. The last thing I need is for them to have ammunition for when this is over and you're no longer hanging around. I'll get the 'why did you scare him off' lecture."

Before Devon could respond, she turned and rushed into the classroom. Her? Out of his league? Scare him off? What kind of men had this girl dated? Man, she doesn't know her own appeal. Her smile alone turns him on. He needed to remember that she's a job, and he needed to act professional. She's just a job. Maybe if he told himself that over and over again, he'd start to believe it. All the guys she dated in the past had nothing to do with this current case. He wasn't sure why the thought of her with another man was making him jealous. It was crazy.

The class started just how he remembered a normal college class beginning. The students turned in their homework assignments, took a pop quiz, then got ready for the lesson of the day. That's when all hell broke loose. Mary lifted the projector screen to put notes on the whiteboard, but someone beat her to it. Written on the whiteboard, in what looked like blood, was a message. Crudely written with red splattered all around it, rage was on full display.

I didn't forget you. You couldn't hide forever, little mouse. Ready or not, here I come.

He found her.

Chapter 3

Devon was moving before he even registered the collective gasp from the close to fifty students in the lecture hall. "Everyone out," he yelled. When no one moved, he pulled out his badge, held it up, and he yelled, "FBI! Out! Now!" That got them moving. In a blink of an eye, he was up next to Mary. She turned and put her head into his chest, trembling in fear. Instinctively, he put one arm around her shoulder and pulled her in tight against his body. With his free hand, he pulled out his phone and hit his speed dial. "Matthews, I need you at Georgetown University right away. Bring forensics and backup. It's Yates, he was here. Inform the chief. I want everyone on top of this."

He hung up and put both arms around Mary and held her tight. She was trembling and panting so hard she was having problems catching her breath. "It is going to be okay. I'm here. Nothing is going to hurt you." Without realizing it, he stroked her back, and it seemed to calm her down.

Forcing herself to gain control of her emotions was essential. She wouldn't allow herself to cry over this bastard. "He wants me scared, doesn't he? He wants to show me he can get to me anywhere. Well, screw that. Screw him. You need to catch this bastard, and I'm going to help you." In an instant, a radical change occurred with her demeanor. She was no longer scared. She was pissed. "Until this minute, I've been in denial. Well, no more. I won't play into his sick games. I'll do anything you need to help get him. But you will get him. I don't care if I need to take an ad in the paper and tell him to come get me. He will be caught, and he will pay for ruining my life."

She moved around him and went to walk up the aisle and out of the room. Devon grabbed her arms before she took more than two steps and pulled her back. "I'm not sure how many times we need to go over this, but you don't go anywhere without me. Especially after today. We're going to be so close even when you shower, I'll be the one to hand you the soap. You got it? We'll catch him, but you need to cooperate and listen to my orders. If I need to keep telling you over and over again not to leave my side, I'll handcuff us together. Just see if I don't."

He still had a hold of her arms, and instead of being angry that he was trying to control her, she felt relieved. Everything he was doing was for her safety. She needed to remember that. Every time she became frustrated with the lack of privacy, she'd need to remind herself it was for her safety. Her world was crumbling around her, but she felt a sense of security being close to him, this man she just met. It didn't make sense, but she was thankful. "Agreed. But I do think I'll be able to manage a shower by myself. If I change my mind, you'll be the first one to know. I just wanted to get out of this room and away from the message. Seeing that on my board and being so close to it is making me feel sick. Can we please go wait in my office?"

Devon looked back at the message and quickly agreed. He didn't even stop to think about how being near the message would affect Mary. "Yeah, let's go to your office and wait for Matthews. Since there's only one door in and out of the classroom, we'll lock it up, so nothing is disturbed before forensics can examine it, and I can watch the door from your office. We'll discuss the shower later. Don't get your hopes up that I'll forget."

Mary shot a glance at Devon's face and saw that swoon worthy smile and when he winked at her, she realized he was joking. Now was not the time to wonder if he really would get in her shower. Later, she might put that to the test and invite him.

They waited in her office for about another twenty minutes before Chief Parker came strutting in, pompous and arrogant. Devon rolled his eyes. With this being such a high-profile case, the chief was going to insert himself into every aspect and micromanage all his agents. Matthews was supposed to inform the chief about what was happening, but he should have known the chief would demand to be front and center at the scene. He was becoming thankful he had put him on bodyguard duty. At least it would get him out of the office and away from the chief for a few days. Earlier, when he spoke to Matthews, he said the chief was becoming more annoying than usual, which was very hard to imagine. Even before this high-profile case, the chief would walk around the office looking over everyone's shoulders to see what they were working on. He'd stand next to them while they were on the phone, hoping to catch a tidbit of information he could run to his boss with. Yes, he was happy to be away from that.

"Walker, what have we got?" Parker called out as he left the office and moved out to the hallway.

Devon placed a light hand on Mary's shoulder. "I'll be right back. Don't go anywhere. How about you collect anything you need to teach from home while you wait? After what just happened, that's where you'll be teaching from." She wouldn't argue with him, not yet. She was terrified. And she was, at last, worrying about her safety. Still, she held her composure and wouldn't allow Yates the satisfaction of seeing her tremble.

Devon walked the chief into the lecture hall to where the forensic techs were going over everything with fine-tooth precision. They had already determined the red substance used to write the message was paint and not blood. Mary would be relieved to hear that. "As you can see, Sir, the techs are working hard. Matthews is questioning some of the students and a few of the other agents are questioning some of the other faculty and so far, no one saw anyone out of the ordinary. They even flashed Yates' photo, and nothing."

Chief Parker shoved his hands into his pockets and sighed. "Good, good. Everyone is doing what they should be doing. I'm going to give the director a call. Make sure you bring Ms. Anderson down to the field office so we can get her statement." He turned to walk away.

"Wait, Chief."

Parker stopped and turned. "Yes, Agent Walker?"

"Mary's been through enough today. I'm going to take her home. I'll make sure she's brought to the office tomorrow. Or, I could take her official statement and email it to you. The less exposure she has right now, the safer she'll be. I don't want any media lurking around the office to even get a look at her and possibly start piecing things together. The longer we can keep her name out of the papers, the longer it will take for some reporter to dredge up her past and splatter it all over the front page. We need to keep this quiet as long as possible. Good?"

The chief hesitated. "Get that statement and email it to me tonight, and we'll call it good. Just remember Walker, this is high profile. You stick with her. I was contemplating assigning another agent to take over for you at night, but since you're not married and don't really have a life, then I feel it would be more beneficial if you stay with Ms. Anderson full time. You are one of my best agents, so don't screw this up."

Should he take that as a compliment, or a criticism? Either way, the chief annoyed the hell out of him. How professional was it to bring his personal life into this? Before Walker could even say a word, the chief was already halfway up the aisle. It's not like protesting would make a difference. Oh, Mary was going to love this. In the span of a day, she found out the person who killed her parents was back, and that same person had threatened her. Now all her privacy is really gone. Sure, he warned they'd be spending a lot of time together until they caught Yates, but he didn't think she understood he was serious. And even he thought she'd be able to have a semblance of privacy at night. Maybe a guard outside her door while she slept. Nope. He was there to stay, all day, every day.

Before he made it up the aisle and back to Mary's office, one of the new Agents, Scott, stopped him. "Hey, Walker, where's the witness at? I'd like to take a look at her."

Look? "She's in her office, Scott. Why?"

"Is she really as hot as the boys are saying?"

"Excuse me?" Much to his surprise, Walker found himself quick to anger. "Just get back to work, Scott."

"Yo, she's been the topic of conversation since she was in the office earlier today. I just wanted to see her for myself. Don't be so uptight."

"Drop it, Scott. She is definitely out of your league."

"A man can only dream… and look. Is it true her legs go all the way up to–?"

Agent Scott cut off when he noticed the look on Walker's face. Having worked with him before, he knew that hostile glare, curled lip, and clenched jaw Walker was displaying was not for show. Scott put his hands up in surrender. "Dude, if she's already spoken for, I'm sorry." He turned and scurried away like a rat.

Spoken for? No. He just thought people should talk about her with respect. But why did he care? Before today, he probably would have been just like the rest of the guys and making jokes. She was hot, yes, but why was he getting mad at the other agents for having a little fun? He didn't want to admit to himself that he was becoming protective of Mary after only a few short hours. Protective or possessive? There is something about her, and he didn't quite know what to make of it. He needed to stay focused on keeping her safe. And to do so, he needed as few distractions as possible. Easier said than done. Everything about Mary was a distraction. The way she smiled could melt a glacier. Scott was right, those legs…

He found Mary sitting quietly in her office with her bag at her feet and her hands folded in her lap. Her face was set in resigned sad lines, and her eyes were shining with the threat of tears, but were wiped away in hopes no one would notice. "You ready to go, Mary?"

Lifting her head, devastation reflected on her face. "Yes, I'm ready. One of the other agents said I'd need to go back to your office. Do you think that will take long? I'm suddenly very tired."

He shook his head. "No, I told the chief I'd take your statement at home and email it to him. I'm taking you back to your apartment."

The tension released from her shoulders, and she breathed a sign of release as she visibly relaxed. "Thank you, Devon. That was kind of you."

Mary was quiet during the drive to her apartment. She stared out the window and kept her hands folded on her lap. If it wasn't for her picking at her fingers and twisting her ring, Devon would've thought she was sleeping. "Is everything okay, Mary?"

She turned to look at him, and he could see the sadness in her eyes. How could she be fine after twenty years of having her world turned upside down? He had to commend her for trying to appear all-right, even though she had to be devastated.

"Yeah, I'm okay. I was just remembering my parents. With every major decision I've made for as long as I can remember, I've always asked myself if this decision would make my parents proud of me or not. If I even considered for a moment that they wouldn't be proud, I didn't go down the path I was heading. It made for boring teenage years, but I didn't care. One psychologist my aunt and uncle sent me to, made me keep a journal of every instance where I changed a decision based on how I think my parents would have felt. She was the first doctor to actually help me out. I was just thinking about that right now. How would they react to where my life has landed? Would they be proud of me, or disappointed? It hurts to think they'd be disappointed in me, in any way."

He reached over and placed a reassuring hand on her shoulder. Something as simple as that small touch helped her to relax a little. "Mary, you couldn't have anticipated Yates coming back to D.C. Even the FBI and MPD thought he was long gone from the area, and he wouldn't be stupid enough to come back. What he's doing right now has nothing to do with any path you've taken in your life. Do you understand? Nothing you've done in your life would've impacted anything regarding Yates or his actions. Well, no, that's not completely true. You survived. You're the only one to survive that bastard, and that's why he's targeting you. I'll keep you safe. Please, trust in me. Ok?"

She turned to look out the window again. "Yes, I understand. And I'll try to trust you. Thank you, Devon."

They lapsed into silence again until they pulled up to her apartment building. Devon looked around and even double checked the address she'd given him. This couldn't possibly be where she lived. Her apartment was not what he expected. With how wealthy her uncle was, he expected a penthouse apartment on the top level of some extravagant building. Instead, he pulled up to what looked like a refurbished manufacturing warehouse. "This is really where you live?"

She let out a small chuckle. "You sound like every person I've ever brought here. Yes, this is where I live, and I love it. I wouldn't want to live anywhere else. And this place isn't that bad. It used to be an old mattress manufacturing plant. When it closed down, a local developer made it into affordable apartments. And in D.C. I'll take any help I can get. I'd never be able to afford an apartment closer to downtown in one of those fancy buildings. Professors just don't make that kind of money."

"Couldn't your uncle help you out with housing? Maybe pull some strings to get you into something fancy with a state-of-the-art security system?"

"My aunt and uncle have done more for me than I'll ever be able to pay them back for. They kept me out of the foster system when my parents were killed. My uncle was just starting his career, yet they dropped everything to take care of a messed up little girl. They gave me every opportunity growing up and I'll forever be in their debt. I fight them almost daily to allow me to make my own way in life. Like it or not, I'm a big girl, and I can take care of my own responsibilities. I'm done being a burden to them and to anyone else."

He knew he had struck a nerve. "Mary, I'm sorry. I didn't mean anything by it. If it's any consolation, you've made a great life for yourself, even with everything that happened to you as a child. I have seen adults use childhood trauma as a crutch instead of pushing forward. I'm sure you know about the statistics of trauma victims turning to crime and drugs, but not you." Still feeling bad for doubting her ability to survive on her own without a handout, he quickly changed the subject. "Now, how about you show me around your apartment so I can assess the security? I can have an FBI tech out here today to install some added security measures."

They quickly made their way from the car and into the building. He shouldn't have been so quick to judge. The outside may have looked like a dump, but the inside was amazing. State-of-the-art. The lower level had a gym with equipment rivaling the equipment in his building's gym, a conference room three times the size of the one the FBI had, and a lounge with lots of plush chairs and what looked to be an eighty-inch flat screen TV mounted to the wall every twenty feet. It was a place people could congregate and relax and never need to leave the building. He was a little jealous.

The elevator was top-notch, not at all what he expected. Everything was spotless. When they reached her door, Mary took out her keys to unlock it. Devon reached around her and took her keys from her hands and gave her 'the look.' She rolled her eyes.

"Me first, always." He stepped inside and pulled her into the room. He locked the door, grasped her shoulders and turned her body so it was parallel with the door. Gently, he walked her the few steps backwards until her shoulders were against the door. "You stay here while I check the apartment. This will be the routine every time we leave the apartment and come back if no one else is here. The entire apartment, every room, elevator, car, gets checked before you enter." He gave her a quick glance as he turned away. She was trying not to yell at him. He couldn't help but smile as he went to give the apartment a quick check.

It was a large apartment, but it only took Devon a moment to make sure everything was secure and no one else was there. The wide-open concept was beneficial to keeping sight lines on Mary. There were no long hallways or blind spots from the living room. On the left was a half bath, and to the right was the coat closet. Straight ahead, and to the right, was a spacious living room with a sliding door opening to a balcony. Then came the dining room and kitchen.

Heading back through the living room, the first door Devon opened led to the sparsely furnished spare bedroom with a few personal items. The second door he opened was like a dream come true. Mary's personal office had to have had hundreds of books lined along three of the walls on bookshelves from the floor to the ceiling. Devon always loved to read, he just never seemed to have time since joining the FBI.

The third door he came to was a full bath, but not the main one. Perfectly folded towels and travel-sized toiletries sat on the sink, waiting for guests. The last door was the master bedroom. Glancing around, it was not at all what other women's bedrooms looked like. There wasn't any clutter, and that made him smile. Mary's walk-in closet and private bathroom were also immaculately clean. It was clear she didn't like chaos in her life, and that was something they had in common.

"All Clear," he yelled from the bedroom.

"Okay," she said. "Since you confirmed no one is lying in wait to attack me, you can be on your way. I'm sure you have better things to do than sit around and babysit me all night."

"You're really having a hard time understanding, aren't you? You're not getting rid of me. The only place I'm going is to your sofa." He added, "Just so you understand, even after you are tucked in for the night, I'll still be here on your sofa. Your sofa and I are going to know each other very well by the end of all this."

"So, you're not going to leave at all? Even if I bolt my doors and windows and promise not to leave? And even with my security system in place?"

"Nope, not even for a few minutes. You're not taking this seriously enough, Mary. Yates never should've been able to get into your classroom at the university, but he did, and he wrote that horrible message to you. Do you really think it would be hard for him to get in here if he was determined? The only way for me to be completely sure of your safety is for you to never be more than one room away from me at any time. So get those ideas out of your head that you are sick of the protection the FBI is providing you, and remember what Yates is capable of. You're stuck with me for every hour of every day until we apprehend him. Get used to it."

"So, are you going to be the one to tuck me in at night? Maybe leave some chocolate on my pillow? I think I could get used to that." She teased, trying to save herself from breaking down.

He took a step closer to her. "Do you want me to tuck you in at night?" His eyes sparkling with mischief. He wondered how riled he could get her.

"Oh, um," she sputtered out. Ugh, was that the best she could come up with? Reaching up, she rubbed her temples. He must have thought she was a total, blithering idiot. As soon as she met his eyes, she knew he was teasing her. If only… No, she told herself. He's here to do a job and only a job. She needed to distance herself or she'd surely get her heart broken once he left. And he would leave. She needed to clear her head and gather her thoughts. Dinner, yes, she could think about dinner, or a drink, a very large stiff drink. Maybe whisky. "Are you hungry?"

She didn't even realize that he had already moved away from her and was across the room. He settled on the sofa, having removed his jacket and shoes, and propped his feet up on the coffee table. "Absolutely. I'm a man, we're always hungry. It's hard-wired in our genes."

She watched him for a moment before moving to the side of the sofa. "Are you comfy enough? Do you need me to get you anything? Extra pillows, a beverage perhaps?"

He didn't even open his eyes to answer. "A beer sounds great. You may need to tell me where you got this couch. It feels like a cloud."

She laughed. "I never took the time to notice. It always felt like a sofa to me, not a cloud. However, I don't have any beer, too many carbs. It's either wine or whiskey. What are you hungry for? But in full disclosure, I'm not a good cook. I've never really learned how to cook, except for the occasional ramen noodle or popcorn. Multiple people attempted to teach me in college, but it didn't work out very well. After almost burning down two different dorm kitchens, I threw in the towel. However, I do have a drawer full of takeout menus."

That got his attention. He stood up from the sofa and looked towards her kitchen. "Make me a list of anything you need, and meals you like. I'll send Matthews to get some groceries. Don't worry, I can cook.

I actually find it therapeutic. But just so you know, I don't do dishes." He held his hands up and wiggled his fingers. "Matthews would never let me live it down if I showed up to work with dishpan hands."

Mary let out a booming laugh, which was the reaction Devon was hoping for. "Really though, I hate dishes. That's why I have a state-of-the-art dishwasher in my apartment and there is not one thing in my kitchen that can not be washed in it. So, I'll cook and load the dishwasher. If you agree to wash anything you won't allow me to put in there. Agreed?"

She wouldn't give in easily. She needed him to sweat a little. "How about this? If the food tasted half as good as your ego makes it out to be, then we have a deal. The deal will be, you cook, and I'll clean. I have my doubts, just so you know. I'm thinking we'll be eating a lot of freezer meals."

She could see the fire in his eyes from across the room. "You'll live to regret those words, sweetheart. Freezer meals, my butt. One more thing while Yates is out there, no more takeout unless it gets picked up by one of our agents. I don't want strangers coming to your door. Got it? If the doorbell rings, you don't answer it. Ever. If you do need someone to drop something off, clear it with me first. And sorry, no friends or other acquaintances. I'll be able to keep tighter security with fewer people around."

"Geez, is there anything I am allowed to do?"

"Now that you mention it, we need to talk about your schedule. I know you want to keep teaching, but after today, I think it would be best to let your TA finish out the term. You can communicate with everyone from here, but I would rather keep you off campus as much as possible. It's for your safety. I hope you understand."

"Is there any use arguing with you? Will you change your mind?"

"None. I always win."

She would see about that. She'd let him win this round because she knew he was right about her safety. Determined, she'd find a way to win next time.

Chapter 4

They weren't even home an hour when Devon broke his rule about no takeout. His stomach growled so loud he was sure she could hear it from across the room. It only took him a moment of mental debate to get up and ask, "Which drawer has the takeout menus?"

She used all her self-control and pressed her lips together to stifle a laugh. "Top drawer closest to the fridge."

He let out a low whistle as he opened the drawer. Crammed full, there were so many menus, Devon could hear tearing as they caught on the sides and top of the drawer. Placing a stack on the counter, he quickly flipped through them, amazed by the variety. "You really have every kind of food you could want in this area. Do all these places deliver?"

"Yep. It may not look like we're close to much, but we're right in the middle of all those delivery areas. Right in the middle of food heaven."

He held up a Chinese menu. "This sound okay?"

After glancing at the menu he was holding up, she quickly spouted off her order. "Sure. Please, just order me a number three with white rice and an order of sweet and sour soup. Give them my name. They know the address."

He looked at her with raised eyebrows. "You really do order out a lot, don't you?"

"I told you I can't cook. I usually pick something up on the way home from my last class. Most of the restaurants know my order by my name. During the day, I eat breakfast in the school cafeteria, and lunch at one of the food trucks that park on campus. So again, no cooking on my part. I usually only keep snack foods in my cabinets."

An hour and a half later, after a very satisfying meal, they placed the dishes in the dishwasher and returned to the sofa.

"Devon, are you married?" The question came out of nowhere.

"No," he said succinctly, trying to keep any trace of humor from showing on his face.

"Me either," Mary said, turning a delicate shade of scarlet.

"I already knew you weren't married. Mary, why are you so nervous? I'd like for you to feel comfortable with me. We're going to be locked in this apartment together for the foreseeable future."

"I'm not," she balked. "Why would I be nervous?" It was an obvious lie, but he didn't need to know that.

Devon shrugged, not wanting to explain her tells, like the way she played with her ring or picked at her nails when she was nervous. After being in her company less than a day, he already noticed some of her little quirks. Reading people was part of his job, and he's damn good at it.

Not wanting to embarrass herself further, she decided escaping was her best option. "Well, I think I'm going to turn in for the night. I have a spare bedroom you can use; you don't need to sleep on the couch."

He shook his head. "Your spare room is in the opposite direction from your bedroom. The sofa puts me between your front door and your room. If someone would break-in during the middle of the night, they would need to go through me before they got to you. But don't worry about me. I don't think I'll be uncomfortable. Like I said before, this is like a cloud. I'll be fine. If you need anything, come and get me, no matter how small." An impish grin spread across his face. "I guess out of consideration for your feelings, I'll make the ultimate sacrifice and sleep with clothes on. Goodnight, Mary."

She stared at him, dizzy as the reality of the day sank in. So much had happened and the danger of it all was finally feeling real. Though he'd told her multiple times it was real, she struggled to believe it. She didn't want to believe it and it wasn't until he explained how he'd put himself in danger to protect her, did she accept it. Not once had she considered the dangers of his job. If something happened to him, could she forgive herself? Was Yates truly back in D.C. because of her? Was it too much to hope it was nothing but a huge coincidence?

Stop being stupid Mary, of course he was back because of you. He even said as much when he vandalized your damn classroom. All those agents are trying to find him and stop him, and any of them could be injured or killed. This was all her fault. She never should have come back to D.C.

"Mary, are you alright?" She wasn't sure how long he was standing next to her. He gently placed his hand on her shoulder and tilted her head so he could look her in the eyes. "I won't let anything happen to you. This is my job, and I'm damn good at it. Trust me, okay?"

While it was his job to put his life at risk, she'd do everything in her power to make sure his proximity to her didn't cause him harm. She would do her job too, dissecting the brains of serial killers and figuring out what makes them tick. Mary had never tried to with Yates because she didn't know if she could mentally handle it. But that wouldn't stop her. She was going to learn every little detail about that crazy son of a bitch, even if it drove her over the edge doing it. No one else was going to be hurt by him.

Without answering him, she put her head down and slowly backed away. "Good night, Devon."

He watched her walk to her room and close the door. Something was wrong, and he wasn't sure what it could be. He'd let her get a good night's sleep, then he would try to figure her out in the morning. He did one more pass through the house, checking all the doors and windows to make sure they were secure. By the time he sat back down, he was just in time for the sports center on TV. He glanced back at her bedroom door once more. An uneasy feeling washed over him. It was like nothing he ever felt before. He needed to figure her out, and soon. He didn't like not being in total control of everything, and that included his thoughts and feelings. If only Matthews could hear him now. Devon needed to clear his head and focus on what was important. Basketball, not his damn feelings.

Chapter 5

Devon woke up around two a.m. to the sound of noises coming from Mary's room. Having a clear view of the front door and her bedroom, he knew no one had come inside, but wanted to check on her. Just in case. Being as quiet as possible, he checked the door and windows as he made his way down the hall to the master bedroom.

Gripping the doorknob firmly, he tried to move it as slowly as possible to limit the creaking. The darkness felt eerie, almost heavy, until a single whimper rang out. The noises Devon heard were Mary in what looked to be the middle of a very vivid nightmare. Slowly moving to the side of her bed, he turned on her lamp. As soon as it clicked, she jumped out of bed and lunged at him, both landing on the floor.

She moved fast, despite having just been asleep. He grabbed her around the shoulders, pulled her in tight so he'd take the impact as they hit the floor, and yelled, "Mary! Mary, damn it. Stop fighting me. It's Devon."

Suddenly, Mary went limp in his arms and slowly opened her eyes. If he hadn't had a hold on her, her head would've slammed against the floor. "Devon, what are you doing in my room? Is everything okay? Did something happen?"

47

"I heard some noises coming from in here and came to make sure you were okay. I think you were having a nightmare. When I turned on the lamp, you tried to attack me. I'm sorry if I startled you. Do you want me to get you anything? Water? Something a little stronger?"

Embarrassed, she whispered, "Oh my goodness. I'm so sorry, Devon. I don't know why I did that. Are you okay? Did I hurt you? I'm so sorry."

He lifted her back onto the bed and sat her down on the edge. "That must have been some nasty dream. Do you want to talk about it? Sometimes talking about it can help, and I'm a very good listener."

"I don't know what you mean. I wasn't having a bad dream." Even as she said it, she couldn't meet his eyes knowing what she was saying was a complete lie, and he knew it, too.

He figured she didn't want to tell him what the dream was about. After the day she had, he'd be surprised if she didn't have nightmares. "Okay. At least let me go get you a glass of water, then you can get back to bed."

Bed? How was she going to get back to bed after a dream like that? It was about Yates again, but not about what he did to her family. It was about what he would do to Devon if he got in his way of taking his revenge on her. She was going crazy. She felt a need to protect him. Mary wasn't sure why or what those feelings of protectiveness were, but something was there. Especially since he was already a dominating figure in her dreams. It had to be stress and the fact Devon had practically taken over her life, for the time being.

She ran her hands down her sides and realized she had sweated through her nightshirt. Moving towards her dresser, she stripped off her shirt, threw it in the hamper, and was pulling out another one when Devon returned to the room with the glass of water. He came to a dead stop inside the door. She looked over her shoulder, not expecting him to have come back so quickly. A flirtatious grin spread across her lips. "Oh! Sorry, I thought I had more time and wanted to change." To stop herself from bursting into laughter, she turned back to face the dresser.

With her back to him, there was nothing too revealing for him to see. That didn't stop his body from reacting as if she was standing in front of him without a stitch of clothing on. He needed a cold shower. Without a word, he moved to her nightstand, set the glass of water down, turned, and left the room. He turned back one more time to give her a quick glance and found she was still watching him, and the embarrassment spread over his face.

Seeing the redness in his cheeks made her feel a little better. Before she could stop herself, she gave him a flirty wink, and her heart pounded with happiness when he grumbled as he walked out the door. One small victory at a time.

Chapter 6

The next morning, after much arguing, Devon reiterated there was no way he'd let Mary go to the campus. And as a result, Mary threw herself into her work, and went into full-on research mode. Luckily, she had most of her research material on-hand in her home office. The information she had gathered over the years was a mixture of her professional opinions and snippets of police files she photocopied off her uncle's desk after he obtained them from the police to have his own people try to track down Yates. Looking over her bullet points, she'd start with the facts she already knew, then work to fill in the blanks.

It was public knowledge that Yates was a family annihilator serial killer. Now if only she could figure out how he chose his targets and what made him tick. She'd try to find any connections he had with the families he murdered and see if there was any overlap between them. That may give her a clue as to how they were selected, and that was the key to the FBI capturing him. The smallest detail could finally end his reign of terror. Yes, the FBI from around the country had been working on this case for years, but none of them had as much to lose as she did. That was her motivation.

After coming up with a plan of action and making her morning coffee, she begrudgingly contacted her teaching assistant and informed him that for at least the next few weeks, he'd be in charge of all her classes. She hung up and sat back in her chair. Rubbing her temples at the thought of another futile argument with Devon, she was certain would come, eventually. He was a stubborn man. It was completely unreasonable that he wouldn't let her go back to the university. Luckily, Markus, her TA, was up for the challenge of finishing her classes for the term. To say it excited him to lead the class was an understatement. She actually thought she heard him squeal a little when she gave him the news. He was in the lecture hall when she got the message from Yates and mentioned some students were worried about returning.

Worried about the threat on the board, or worried about being in proximity to her? Either way, being near her automatically placed someone in danger. And putting her students even remotely in danger was not acceptable. From what she read about Yates; he wouldn't worry about inadvertently harming bystanders if they tried to actively interfere with his heinous crimes.

She instructed her TA to offer to live stream the class for those who didn't feel comfortable attending in person. She never had to worry about attendance in her classes before. After she sent over all her notes and tests for the next couple of weeks, she got down to business, pulling information on Yates. For a person who dominated a good portion of her life, she knew only the basics about him, all things considered. But she was determined to change that.

Devon poked his head into her office multiple times throughout the day to check on her and ask if there was anything she needed. Once, he came around her desk to see what she was working on, but she closed her screens and pulled up something for one of her classes. Mary explained how she was gathering information for her TA. She wasn't sure why, but she didn't want him to know she was researching Yates. Was she worried he'd try to stop her? Maybe. Or maybe she wanted to feel like she had control over one small aspect of her life, even if it was just research. But why not ask for his help? No, she already knew he was involved up to his ears, but she couldn't shake the feeling of dread when she thought of Devon's safety. She'd keep Devon in the dark for as long as possible.

Getting the files on Yates without Devon finding out turned out to be the hard part. The only mail he didn't insist on checking were the packages from her aunt and uncle, and that was only because her uncle had one of his security guards hand-deliver them. However, Devon didn't trust her uncle's security guard and had Matthews run a background check on him before he'd even allowed him to set foot in Mary's apartment. After that, he no longer gave him a hassle when he showed up at the door.

After many failed attempts in the past to obtain information by her own requests, Mary decided to use her uncle's contacts and not the FBI or police department. It would also be beneficial to stay away from filing information requests with the FBI or police department because it would get back to Devon. Every time she'd call them, her aunt, uncle, and his head of security peppered her with warnings about digging too deep, and she didn't need to hear the same nagging from him.

Her uncle picked up on the second ring. "Hello, Mary. How is solitary life? Is there anything we can send you to help make it a little more peaceful?"

"Uncle Robert, can you please break me out of here? What I need is fresh air. I need to teach."

"Tsk-Tsk. Now Mary, as much as it annoys you, you know the FBI only has your safety at hand. And it's only the second day. So, really, do you need any groceries, books, pamper items your aunt can go shopping for?"

"Well, now that you mention it, since you seem to be in an accommodating mood, do you think you'd be able to use one of your contacts and have them get me copies of all the FBI and police files on Yates?" She rushed out in a single breath.

The silence on the other end of the phone. "Mary Anderson. What the hell are you thinking? Put agent Walker on the phone."

"Uncle, calm down." Mary tried saying in her sweetest voice. "I'm not getting into trouble. You know how my brain works. I need to learn more about him or I'll go crazy. Help me, please."

"You need a keeper; you know that girl. Patricia and I worry about you every second of every day. How do you think this is going to make her feel when I tell her what you are asking of me? And don't you dare even ask me to keep this from her."

"You know I'd never ask that of you, uncle Robert. Not like you'd listen, anyway. You and aunt Patricia gossip like teenage girls. I know she's going to worry, but you know she'll understand. She helped me study for every step of my education. She knows why I do what I do. Will you please think about helping me gather this information?"

"Will you think about looking for a husband?"

Luckily, he couldn't see her roll her eyes through the phone. "You know what year it is, right? A woman is perfectly capable of living a rewarding and fulfilling life without a husband in her life trying to micromanage her. Me, I'm one of those women."

A huff that could tumble a house resounded through the phone. "Fine, young lady, you win. But once this is all over, since you refuse a husband, I'm hiring you a maid, a cook, a security guard, and a chauffeur. If you agree to that, then I'll make sure you get your information. Agreed?"

"How about one person who can do it all? That is all the intrusion I'll agree to. And none of them are live-in."

"You drive a hard bargain. At least I taught you something. We love you, Mary."

"I love you too, uncle Robert."

Mary tried to be independent, and while her aunt and uncle understood her unwillingness to accept help, it didn't deter them from trying all the same. Though her uncle made certain Mary could defend herself, he also believed a husband would increase the chances she wouldn't work herself to death. Something he was sure she would do, and that's why they pushed the topic often.

She was the first to admit she was a workaholic, and although she also worked out every day, her diet wasn't the best. When she remembered to eat, it was all about comfort food. If she wasn't able to get her Chinese food, it was either food truck lobster rolls or Vietnamese banh mi sandwiches. At this point in her life, she didn't have the time or desire for a husband. From past experiences, a husband would impede on what she wanted to accomplish. Coming close to marriage four years ago helped her to realize how much of a strong, independent woman she really is. After two years of dating, Shawn proposed, and Mary thought it was magical. That was, until she surprised Shawn at work with an early lunch, and walked in on him and his secretary going at it on his desk. That day, she realized she was perfectly fine on her own. Having a husband or boyfriend was sure to end in heartbreak. She was more than happy to focus on her work for the time being.

She was lying to herself. The real reason she didn't want a family was because she believed she'd never be able to escape her past. After all the stories about her in the papers, and having her name dropped in movies and tv shows about what happened to her family, she'd never subject anyone else to that kind of intrusiveness. She knew she wouldn't be able to survive having someone like Yates target any more of her loved ones. No, she was perfectly fine living alone, being the only target in his sights.

Knowing what she was doing in her office was taking a toll on her sleeping and eating, he wanted to remove her from the situation and try to lighten the mood. Spending the night having a nice dinner and some conversations were his real motives, but he'd play it aloof. It was around eight p.m. when Devon poked his head into her office.

"Hey, I haven't seen you come out in a while. Are you ready for a break?"

Slightly shaking her head, she said, "no, I think I'm just going to head to bed. Working on all these lesson plans has given me a headache."

Devon knew damn well that Mary wasn't working on any lesson plans. He didn't mean to eavesdrop, but this morning he was coming to ask her if she wanted breakfast, and overheard her on the phone with Markus. Fortunately, she was handing over her class to him for the term. That would save Matthews the trip later. Devon and Matthews discussed that very decision early this morning. The threat against Mary was too much of a risk to allow her near vulnerable students.

One look at Devon's face, and Mary knew he wasn't believing her headache excuse. Trying to act nonchalant, she stood, stretched, faking exhaustion from her work. Hoping that would make her story of a headache appear true. Her stomach gurgled and growled, betrayed, as she caught a whiff of something cooking in the kitchen. Her stomach rumbled again, so loud that Devon heard it from across the room. He laughed, holding the door open, and thumbed back towards the kitchen. Knowing he wouldn't accept the rejection sizzling on her tongue, she gracefully conceded to dinner. Afterwards, she'd quickly retire to her room for much needed rest. It had been a long, tiring day, and she hadn't learned nearly enough yet about Yates.

Mary didn't make it back to her room until two a.m., but every second of missed sleep was worth it for the night she had. Dinner was nothing short of a masterpiece. They started off with an avocado caprese salad and a mango, and grilled shrimp crostini for the appetizers. The main course was duck breasts with apricot chutney on a bed of jasmine rice and candied carrots. Yum! He even made one of her favorites for dessert. Chocolate chip cookies. She, however, had absolutely no room to take another bite and would save those for tomorrow with her morning coffee.

Clearing the plates away in total silence was bothering Mary, but she didn't want to go to bed yet, so if she could get him talking, it would give her a reason not to retire to her room. "Devon, I think you missed your calling when you decided to join the FBI. I admire why you joined, but I think you were destined to become a chef. Don't you realize you could make a killing as a personal chef, especially here in D.C.? People would pay top dollar for someone like you to cook their meals. And if you get bored with the slow pace, you could double as a security guard."

A dish sponge went flying in front of her face. "You think you're so funny, don't you, you cheeky woman?"

"I know I'm hilarious. My students tell me all the time. Well, kind of? They tell me I'm hilarious, mostly after they receive grades or homework assignments. So, I'm not sure exactly how to interpret that."

Looking around, she located the sponge by the sofa. Tossing it back to Devon, Mary moved to make herself comfortable in Devon's spot before he finished the dishes. Maybe she'd be able to find a movie for them to enjoy instead of watching sports.

The idea of a movie went out the window when the first channel Mary turned on was the news. The image on the screen made bile rise in her throat. Front and center on the screen, *Infamous serial killer Jimmy Yates back on the rampage in D.C.*

An arm came around her from behind and took the remote out of her hand. "Yeah, I don't think so. No news tonight. I think sports center is on. How about that?"

Mary just nodded.

Devon and Mary were sitting in silence when he noticed she was playing with her ring again. She seemed to do that when she was nervous or scared. "Mary, tell me about your ring."

She looked at him, confused. "My ring? Why do you want to know about my ring?"

He reached over and grabbed her hand, pulling it close to get a better look. "Because the ring seems special to you, and I want to know everything about you. So, I'd really like to know about this ring."

Dang, he's so sweet. Her cheeks turned scarlet. "Well, yes, this ring is very special to me. It was my mother's. My mother grew up rather poor, but my grandparents tried to go above and beyond on special occasions. The ring may not look like much, but the stone is real. My grandfather set aside as much money as he could every month for almost a year to be able to give this to her. They gave her this ring on her sixteenth birthday. It was one of her most cherished possessions until the day she died. She was actually wearing it when Yates murdered her. She never took it off. My aunt and uncle told me all the special memories about the ring. Since I was so young when they were killed, I just remember it being a pretty object on mommy's finger. When looking back at photo albums of when I was a baby, in more than one photo, it looked like I was trying to eat the ring."

She took a moment to gather her thoughts, taking a deep breath. "My aunt and uncle made sure to get it back from the coroner so they could give it to me. They wanted to do something very special with it, so they gave it to me on my sixteenth birthday. They waited until I was old enough to understand how special it was. That's when they told me about how sentimental it was to my mother. They were worried I'd freak out about it since my mother was wearing it when she was murdered, but that didn't matter to me. This is my connection to her, and I'll never take it off. Anytime I need reassurance about anything, or I'm feeling stressed or nervous, I just reach down and touch it and it centers me again. When I'm touching it, I try to think about how my mother would handle whatever situation I found myself in. This ring keeps me grounded."

"It's great that you have something like that to remember your mother by. Cherish it, but don't let it make you sad. When you touch it, remember all the joyful memories your aunt and uncle told you about the ring." Without thinking, Devon picked up her hand and placed a gentle kiss on the top.

Scarlet flooded her cheeks. Jumping from the sofa, she walked over to the stereo against the wall. What they needed as a distraction was music. "What kind of music do you like to listen to, Devon? I'm guessing classical."

He didn't respond. She turned to look at him and noticed how somber his expression was. Maybe he didn't like her joke. Fine, she'd put on her favorite artist, and if he didn't like it, too bad. Moments later, *Highway to Hell* by AC/DC sang throughout her apartment. That seemed to get his attention.

"AC/DC, huh?"

"Yup. My number one band." Feeling a little brave, she teased him with some truth. "And you know what?"

"No, what?"

"When I'm all alone, and in the shower. I like to sing AC/DC and imagine they are singing just for me. *Dirty Deeds Done Dirt Cheap* is a good song for shower time."

Giving him that information was the biggest mistake she's ever made. For the next hour, Devon played it over and over again. "Mary, you aren't like any woman I've ever met. You love rock music, you're kind-hearted and intelligent. I can have a decent conversation with you and not have fashion and makeup be brought up once. You don't even give me crap about watching sport. Dang."

She wasn't sure if the list he was reciting was good or bad, but he laughed about it, so she figured it was a good thing.

59

Noticing the time, Mary called a halt to the mocking for the evening. "As much as I'm having a blast. I'm going to head to bed. You feel free to stay up and enjoy the music. Good night, Devon."

"Good night, Mary."

Chapter 7

The sun was shining through the curtains as Mary stirred awake. Memories of last night flooded back. She hadn't had such a relaxing night in months. She and Devon spent hours talking, laughing, and genuinely enjoying each other's company.

Now it was a new day, and she saw Devon in a new light. Smiling, she made her way to the bathroom for a shower. Devon must have heard her moving around, because as she walked out of the bathroom and into her bedroom, he was leaning against her door frame with a cup of hot coffee in his hands. He was wearing a plain, almost fitted, white t-shirt, and a pair of old FBI basketball shorts. His hair looked like he just rolled out of bed. Someone shouldn't look so good first thing in the morning. Unceremoniously, she stopped dead in her tracks.

"Coffee?" He asked with a big smile on his face. Moving away from the door, he walked to meet her in the middle of the room.

"Yes, please." Gently taking the cup out of his hands, she tried to avoid looking him in the eyes. She failed. Gosh, his eyes were gorgeous. He had the most captivating sea-green eyes a girl could get lost in. She was so busy gawking at him, she almost let her towel drop to the floor. As it started to unwind, she frantically grabbed the edges, fumbling and almost dropping her coffee. Devon was quicker and snatched the cup out of her hand so she could grab her towel.

Her cheeks blazed in embarrassment. What didn't help was Devon moved to her nightstand, set the cup down, and turned towards the door, all the while whistling *Dirty Deeds Done Dirt Cheap* by AC/DC. Mary wanted to throw something at him, but the only thing she had on was her towel, and that wasn't coming off until he was out of her room. Unlike the other night, this time she'd make sure her door was closed before getting dressed.

Devon had breakfast waiting for her when she finally walked out of her room. She wore a comfy pair of palazzo pants and one of her uncle's old long-sleeved campaign shirts. Devon had also changed and was in a pair of jeans and a plain black t-shirt. Even dressed down, he looked absolutely amazing. The t-shirt was snug, accentuating the muscles in his arms and shoulders. Damn. She was in trouble. It had been so long since she'd felt attracted to a man. Why did her body react this way now with her babysitter? The man that wouldn't give her another glance if it were not for his job. Her brain didn't care about those reasons. All it was telling her to do was throw him on the bed and tear his clothes off. Devon hadn't seen her yet, as she turned around and walked back to her room.

Thirty minutes later, Mary returned to the kitchen.

"What took you so long? I thought you were coming right out, so I made breakfast. I had to throw the first batch away, since it got cold. You do not want to eat cold eggs."

"I got another shower?" She whispered miserably.

The humor in his eyes didn't extend to his voice, for once. "Oh yeah. Two showers? Are you good? Are you ready for breakfast? I'm making my Specialty."

"Yes, please. Breakfast sounds amazing. What are you honoring me with today?"

"Today, my dear, we are having eggs benedict on whole wheat English muffins and a glass of orange juice." Devon whirled his spatula around in the air as he told her the menu.

It was absolutely heavenly. She was not looking forward to going back to toast and a diet coke for breakfast, or a quick bite off the campus food truck once he was gone.

After breakfast, she asked him to teach her some cooking tricks, but he gave up only five minutes into the first lesson. She was attempting to make a vodka sauce for shrimp and lobster stuffed shells they were going to have for dinner when she dumped vodka over the pan onto the burner and almost caught her kitchen on fire. That's when he told her to stick to takeout. No matter how much pleading Mary did, he wouldn't change his mind on the lessons. Maybe one day, she'd take the cooking class her aunt had begged her to take for years.

After they cleaned the kitchen up, Devon refused to let her run back to her office. He adamantly insisted he was bored, and he needed her entertainment. Apparently, his idea of entertainment consisted of playing cards for the rest of the morning. They played everything from go-fish to phase-10 and ended with him teaching her poker. Or so he thought.

Mary refused to play for money, so she walked over to her pantry and pulled out a family size bag of M&M's. "This is the currency for the games tonight. Take it or leave it."

Letting out a booming chuckle, Devon said, "M&M's are for children. Why don't we play for articles of clothing? Unless you know you'll lose and be too embarrassed when you're sitting naked at your own kitchen table."

"No, it's not that I'll be too embarrassed. I just really like M&M's. Please?" She asked with mischievousness in her voice.

Little did he know at the time how thankful he would be for that. She ended up being a card shark and took him for all his M&M's. If she'd agreed to play for clothing, he'd have been down to his birthday suit in only a few hands.

Devon finally called a stop to the card games when Mary had damn near the entire bag on the plate in front of her. He was in a bad mood; he hated losing. What made it worse was her sitting across from him casually popping M&M's into her mouth with a huge smile on her face. He'd been conned, but he'd get her back. Looking up at the clock, he realized the baseball game was about to start. He'd make Mary sit with him to watch the game. That would serve as a small payback. She thought baseball was the most boring sport he watched. She's made that clear more than once in the last two days.

It brought him great pleasure when Mary groaned as he turned on the Washington Nationals game. They were playing the Phillies, and the game was only at the top of the second inning, so there was a lot more game to watch. Finally, being able to let his guard down slightly, Devon relaxed and admitted he was a little tired. He closed his eyes for a moment and listened to the announcer.

As soon as his breathing evened out, Mary knew he was asleep. She'd keep the TV on and headed to her room for a nap. Even though Devon told her so many times how her sofa was so comfortable, she really didn't want to fall asleep there with him on the other side.

Removing her pants to get more comfortable, she was finally ready for a short afternoon nap. She barely climbed into bed and snuggled under the covers before slipping into a deep sleep.

Mom!

Mary's eyes flew open, tears streaming down her face, and her heart pounding like it was trying to release itself from her chest. She shook her head, trying to clear the rest of the drowsiness. The images of her dream were still vivid in her mind. They were always so vivid. She'd had the same nightmare for the last twenty years, and it didn't show any sign of going away. Even after all the years of therapy.

Facelessness. Blood. Death. Horror.

She sat up slowly, reminding herself it was only a dream. But it was *the* dream. It was so devastatingly real, just like it was happening all over again. Since Devon came into her life, she'd been remembering more bits and pieces of what happened the night her parents died. They were the details her mind had kept hidden all those years, but they were finally coming to the surface. Those details were adding themselves to her recurring nightmares, making them even more terrifying. It was like the safety walls her mind built to protect her from the pain were crumbling. She didn't know how much more she'd be able to handle.

Mary kept reminding herself it was only a dream. She needed light. With her blackout curtains she couldn't see but a few feet in-front of her face. Her trembling hand reached out to turn on her bedside lamp. It took three tries to hit the switch on the lamp and illuminate her room.

65

Her shirt was soaked through with sweat, and her mouth was so dry it felt like she'd stuffed it full of cotton.

The pain washing over her was overwhelming. It was the same pain that dominated every night and the dream she had since she was a child. The doctors tried what seemed like every sleeping pill ever created to help her with the nightmares, but nothing stopped the terror from ambushing her in her sleep.

Staggering to the bathroom, she turned the shower on cold. She didn't want to speak about the dream, and she knew if she went to the kitchen to get a drink, Devon would wake up and know something was wrong the moment he saw her face. He was such a light sleeper. She got some water from her bathroom sink before she jumped into the shower. The cold water rained down on her and woke her up, but did nothing to help the shaking. Her shaking, however, wasn't from the cold, it was from memories. She took her time in the shower, hoping it would help her calm down. It didn't, and she decided to get out and go back to work. Work was the one thing that distracted her from everything else around her.

On the way out of her bathroom, she sensed she was no longer alone in her bedroom. For a brief second, she worried someone had gotten into her apartment. But that couldn't be possible with Devon situated on the sofa between her bedroom and the front door. Even if he was still taking a nap, he'd wake up with the intrusion.

Walking out of the bathroom revealed her feeling of another presence was true. Devon was sitting on the side of her bed, watching her. He looked amazing, and surprisingly wide awake. As soon as recognition hit her, the tension in her shoulders relaxed. It seemed every time she found him in her bedroom; she didn't have any clothes on. "I'm sorry. I didn't mean to wake you."

He studied her face. "Mary, it's three in the afternoon. I shouldn't be sleeping, anyway. Are you okay? I was surprised to hear the shower going, since you already had two showers this morning." Concern filled his voice.

Knowing he could read her like a book, she decided not to lie. "No, I'm not okay, but I will be. I decided to take a nap and had a bad dream." She walked to the closet while wrapping her hair up into the towel to stop it from dripping down her back.

"Just a bad dream? It looks to me like it was more of a nightmare. You're shaking so much I can hear your teeth chattering from over here. Do you want to talk about it?" He wanted to get up and wrap her in his arms, but she still looked terrified. He thought better of it and decided to give her a few moments. Seeing her in this state made him want to take her away and never let anything harm her again, but he wasn't sure why.

She moved further into her closet until she all but disappeared. The only part of her body visible to Devon was her pert, little backside. It shook as she pushed clothes aside, trying to find something to wear. That little movement was so erotic he couldn't suppress a soft groan.

"No, thank you. I really would rather not talk about it. The night-mare is done and gone, and it won't come back tonight," she called from inside the closet.

He chuckled. "You won't dream because you 'will it' so?"

"Yes, because I 'will it' so," she replied, sounding exasperated. "Why don't you go back to the living room to watch your sports? I'm just going to read a little and try to relax until dinner."

He called her bluff. "No, you're not. You're going to either sit here and brood over the nightmare, or you'll sneak over to your office to work." He knew he hit it on the mark when she peeked out of the closet, and a frown appeared on her face. He needed to draw her attention to something else. "Why don't we go to the living room and watch a movie? I might even let you pick."

She let out a hearty laugh and peeked her head out of the closet again to look at him. "In the few days you've been here, not once have you let me pick what was on my TV. I doubt today would be any different. You're a guy. Guys seem to think that it's encoded in their DNA that no one else is allowed to take control over the remote besides them. He who controls the remote controls the world, right?"

"Exactly. The reason I haven't allowed you to pick what we watch is that you always watch boring shows. I like shoot 'em up, action movies. You pick romcoms or documentaries that put me to sleep." Getting up from the bed, he moved to lean against the doorjamb of the closet. He loved watching her and the way she moved, and the towel sliding down her body. Everything she did, she exhibited an elegance he'd never seen before. Nothing about Mary was like the other women from his past. It was refreshing.

Once in the living room, and settled on the couch, he knew he wouldn't be able to let her pick the TV show when she selected one on Helvetica, a documentary about fonts. Lasting only about twenty minutes, he decided he couldn't take any more and got off the sofa and moved towards the balcony. Just as he was closing the door, he heard her let out a whole-hearted laugh. Turning back to look at her, she was facing him and gave him a wink. She loved seeing him frustrated.

Taking pity on him, she walked over to the balcony door, knocked on the window, and pointed over her shoulder at her office. Mouthing 'homework' to him, she turned and walked away. If she moved quick enough, he wouldn't be able to stop her before she made it to her office. For some reason, he was always trying to distract her from working.

Thinking about it, she probably had some schoolwork to finish and send to her TA, but she knew as soon as she went into her office, the mountains of all the information she collected on Yates would pull her attention away from school. She once told him teaching was her main focus, and nothing would distract her from her students. Well, she found a distraction with a pull strong enough to change her mind. A deadly pull. Jimmy Yates.

Glancing towards her office, he knew perfectly well she wouldn't be doing homework. He wished he knew what to say to her to draw her attention elsewhere, but he didn't want to let on that he knew about her crusade to find something to help the FBI. Once she felt comfortable enough to confide in him about her goal, then he'd use any trick he had to defer her attention. But if he told her he knew about the room and what she was doing, he could lose her trust. And losing her trust was unacceptable, not just professionally, but the thought of her not being able to trust him made his chest tighten with pain. But why the dramatic reaction? She was just a job, right?

As soon as the door closed behind her, Mary's mind raced with all the new information she discovered the day before. Sure, she had papers she needed to grade, but that could wait until later. Her TA had been with her for a few years while he's been working on his own doctorate. He was smart, he'd improvise if he needed to.

What was happening to her? Before all this, or even just last week for that matter, she never would've put schoolwork off for any reason. Her career and students kept her moving forward. It's what stopped her from wasting her life by dwelling on Yates and the horror he dealt out over the years, and continued to deal every day so long as he was a free man. He rips apart families and makes nightmares come to life. She wouldn't let him dominate any more of her life than he already had.

She needed to do the schoolwork first, then she'd allow herself to spend the rest of the night dissecting the information her uncle had provided. She couldn't let her own vendetta stop her from contributing to the education of future forensic psychologists. One of her students may very well help with the apprehension of the next Ted Bundy. In her own investigation and compiling of information, she could feel a breakthrough coming. Hopefully, any day now, she'd be able to forward her findings to the FBI.

Chapter 8

The same routine went on every day for two weeks before Mary finally reached her breaking point. Though she was making headway on her exploration into Yates, the crime scene photos and reports were making her sick and wreaking havoc on her nerves. Every day, she forced herself to go into her office and dreaded every moment spent inside. She wasn't sleeping, and only ate when Devon made her set her work aside for a meal, which was three times a day, like clockwork. The food helped, but what she really needed was fresh air. She needed to leave her apartment before she crawled up the wall or slammed her head against the nearest hard surface. The trouble was she had to convince her jailer it'd be okay to go outside. And not just onto the balcony. It isn't up for debate. She was leaving this apartment with or without his permission.

Leaving her office, she went looking for Devon. He wasn't on the sofa where he normally was when she holed up in her office. It wasn't like there were many places in her small apartment where he could be. She went to the kitchen to grab a cold drink and found the room empty. Where was he? It wasn't like him to be anywhere other than in her living room, parked on the couch, as he had been for two weeks. He refused to take a day off, or even leave her for more than a few hours, and never without telling her before leaving. During those hours away, his partner sat in her living room or walking around the apartment, making her anxious. Devon was the last person she saw every night before bed, and the first person she saw when she woke up each morning. He was really growing on her.

Even though she locked herself away with her work, Devon made sure she came out and shared meals with him. He used the excuse that people shouldn't eat alone. She was the first to admit he was an outstanding cook, so she didn't mind the interruptions. Although she would never admit she enjoyed sharing her meals with him, too. He didn't need a bigger ego.

She wondered if it wasn't for him being assigned to babysitting duty. If they met on the street, would he even have given her another glance? Talking to him was so natural, it seemed like it took hours to have a meal. She'd never met anyone, man or woman, who made her feel so at ease. She wasn't even this comfortable with her aunt and uncle, and they raised her. When she made her way out of her kitchen, she still wasn't able to see Devon anywhere. She yelled, "Devon!"

"Out here." He replied from her balcony, reclining on one of the zero gravity chairs he had Matthews pick up. Why he needed them, she had no clue. Her plastic deck chairs were perfectly fine. Devon disagreed.

"Devon, I know you said I needed to stay cooped up, but if I have to stay inside one more moment, I might go crazy."

He looked like he wanted to laugh. He'd wondered how long it would take her to reach this point and had been anticipating this talk for over a week. During the last few days, he could see her staring longingly at the front door. "All you had to do was ask. I told you I wouldn't take you back to the university, or to pick up takeout, but I never said you couldn't leave your apartment. The rules were that wherever you go, I go with you, and I go first." He tried to suppress a smile, but was failing. It was adorable.

"Are you stinking kidding me?" She whispered, with a hint of violence in her voice, as she shot him a murderous glare. "All this time, I thought I was more or less a prisoner in my own home when I could have left at any time?"

"Yes," he said casually. "Well, not anytime, but almost. All you had to do was ask."

"What?" She was expecting a fight. "Really?"

He nodded and was pleased to see it infuriated her even more. "Mary, you look so frustrated. How about I take you to the gym to burn off some of that energy?"

The gym? That sounded like a great idea. "Does the gym happen to have a pool?"

"It has a great pool, and what's even better, is that we'll have it to ourselves. I have connections."

"How are you going to pull that off? Even the FBI shouldn't be able to shut down an entire gym on a whim. That'd be an abuse of power."

"Actually, the FBI can do whatever they want. But this time, I'm going to depend on my father's influence to get what I want. My father has been the superintendent of Georgetown Prep High School for fifteen years. He'll let us use their facilities, and since it's during class time, no one will be using it. So no abuse of power is needed."

A nice long swim was just what she needed to clear her head. Her aunt and uncle have been telling her that for as long as they could remember, Mary was always happiest when she was in any type of water. Running to her room, she changed into workout clothes, grabbed her gym bag and shoved in her bathing suit, goggles, swim cap, and towel. She was ready in less than five minutes.

"Ready, let's go." She exclaimed enthusiastically.

Devon loved to see her excited. It was refreshing. If he had to make a guess, he'd say she was normally a very serious person. Never allowing herself to cut loose and have fun. "We need to swing by my apartment first. I wasn't planning on a swim when I packed for this detail, so I need to grab my suit."

It took them longer than she wanted to get to the gym. Apparently, every move was in the name of safety. And it made her impatient. He had to check the hall in front of her apartment, the elevator, the parking garage, and even under and inside the car. And all of that was before they even left her parking lot. He did those same things when they reached his apartment. She wasn't sure why he would need to 'clear' his apartment. He wasn't the one potentially being stalked by a serial killer, but he did it anyway. Hopefully, Yates didn't even know Devon existed. On the way out, he again checked the hallway, elevator, parking lot and car. This routine was getting old.

Devon's apartment building was exactly what she pictured it to be, too. He lived in a basic high-rise apartment building close to downtown. There was no fancy doorman or chandeliers in the lobby. His actual apartment, on the other hand, was quite different than she expected. While Devon was packing a gym bag, she took a moment to look around. At first glance, it looked like a normal bachelor pad. It had a projection TV that took up an entire wall, and a pinball machine in the living room. It even had a kegerator in the dining room. Really, right in the dining room?

What truly surprised her, but really shouldn't have, was the state-of-the-art kitchen that most chefs probably dream of. It had a refrigerator so big it would probably take up half her bedroom, and an eight-burner gas stainless steel stove with the pot filler in the back so you didn't have to carry pots full of water across the room. It looked like a kitchen out of a catalog.

He came out of his room and caught her ogling his kitchen. "So, you like it?"

"It's absolutely wonderful. Did you pick all this out?"

"Yep. I worked with a renovator and customized it myself."

"Wow." She still couldn't quite close her mouth.

"I can give you the name of my construction guy if you like, but you know a kitchen like this would be lost on you. And before you ask, no, I won't change my mind about giving you cooking lessons. I'm sure I can help you pick out a real fancy drawer to keep all your takeout menus in. We can make them all alphabetized and everything."

She knew he was joking. "Har, har, har. You know, you're not as funny as you think you are." She tried to be completely serious, but failed miserably.

He walked up to her and tousled her hair. "Yes, I am. I'm freaking hilarious and you know it."

Yeah, she knew it, but she would never admit it. He didn't need her to stroke his ego. "Let's go, Mr. Comedian. I want to see this pool you promised me."

The ride to the school was blissfully quiet. It gave Mary time to think to herself, something she felt she had not been able to do lately.

She was looking forward to seeing the school Devon's father worked at, well not really the school, but the pool. A swim was exactly what she needed. She could get lost swimming laps. In college, she spent hours swimming laps to relieve her stress. Her aunt and uncle said she'd always been a little fish. She would rather go to the beach than to places like Disney or even France. Her aunt and uncle did so much for her after they took her in. They even had an indoor/outdoor Olympic sized swimming pool installed at their home in Pennsylvania not long after Mary came to live with them.

They tried to spoil her whenever possible. They were never able to have children of their own, so they doted on Mary. Even though they could give Mary everything she ever wanted, they also instilled discipline and the sense of pride in accomplishing things for yourself.

In grade school, anytime Mary wanted to go to a camp or take a summer course, she tried to come up with a way to earn the money, not just depend on her aunt and uncle. Mary did everything from a lemonade stand to mowing the neighbor's lawns to dog walking, and later babysitting the neighborhood children. She always had to be busy. She didn't want to depend on her aunt and uncle because she feared, at any time, something would take them away from her, too.

She pulled from her thoughts as they came up to the guard shack in front of the school. After a quick ID check, they waved them forward. Out of all the years she's lived in or around the D.C. area, she's never been to Georgetown Prep. The campus was much larger than she expected. Devon didn't park in the main parking lot; but, instead, pulled to a service entrance. After exiting the car and grabbing their bags, he produced an electronic key card from his wallet that opened the door leading to a dark hallway that smelled of familiar chlorine.

Mary and Devon walked into the pool area, and her worries disappeared. The smell of chlorine was an instant stress reliever. Someone should make a candle that smells like a pool. She hadn't been in an Olympic sized lap pool since college. Her body tingled with the electricity of anticipation. Rushing into the locker room after Devon cleared it. Of course, she threw on her suit in record time, but he was still ready before her. She walked out and stopped dead in her tracks.

Devon was on the side of the pool, placing his badge and gun on a small table and moving it next to the water for easier access, if necessary. They didn't need to worry about someone else coming into the pool and seeing the gun. He'd locked all the entry doors. For safety. He had his back to her, and she couldn't look away from his bare muscles. Damn. She knew he was fit, but this is the first time she's seen him partially dressed without a shirt. Water! She needed to get into the water.

He'd heard her come out of the locker room but didn't want her to see him blatantly checking her out. He saw the suit she was planning on wearing. It left little to the imagination. Devon didn't turn around to look at Mary until he heard a splash. Her towel dropped at the end of the pool, and she was gliding through the water with graceful form. And her exquisite little bottom wiggling with every kick. *Come on, man, get it together.* Looking up at the ceiling, he knew he was in trouble. He'd made it two weeks without making a move, but he wasn't sure how much longer he could hold out. She was damn near perfect. Everything a man could ever want in a woman. She wasn't only beautiful, but she was intelligent, strong, fierce, and independent, too. She was the whole package.

From the moment Mary got into the water, everything else disappeared. With each stroke, her worries dissipated, and the only thing left was the fluid motions of her gliding through the water. Concentrating on her breathing and stroke count, nothing else crossed her mind. For her, being in the water was like magic. It didn't matter if the world was crumbling around her. When she was in the pool, she didn't notice anything else. Not the stacks of papers to grade, lessons to plan, looming threats, or Devon watching her every move. There was only her, the water, and one lap after another. 1 – 2 – 3– breathe. 1 – 2 – 3– breathe. For a moment, she was free.

Chapter 9

Devon finally put a stop to the swimming. He moved to block her from making her next turn. Pulling her head up out of the water, Mary looked at the clock. Shocked by the time, she couldn't help but wonder how they'd been in the pool for over two hours. "I'm sorry, you could've stopped me before this. I kinda get into a rhythm and block everything else out."

He slowly shook his head. "You looked like you needed this. You're a machine. It's impressive. You didn't break your stride or slow down in almost two hours. But, to be honest, I got bored after thirty minutes."

She laughed, "thirty minutes, what have you been doing since?"

"Watching you."

She thought he was joking, but when she looked at him, there was no humor on his face. There was something else there, and her heart gave a little flutter. She knew that look. And she felt it, too. Lust. The thing she wanted more than anything was to throw herself into his arms and never let go. Instead, her moronic conscience wouldn't let her act on her feelings.

"Oh," were the only words the mouth could form. Her heart raced. To remove herself from the situation, she quickly exited the pool and wrapped herself in a towel. Why was she suddenly feeling shy? She was determined not to let him see any signs of embarrassment, but that all went out the window when she saw the look of passion on his face, and her breath caught in her chest. Hesitating not a moment longer, she rushed into the locker room to change and head home before the bell rang and announced the end of the school day.

Dinner that night was, for lack of a better word, tense. Not that she would ever act on it. Devon was there to do a job. She had to keep reminding herself of that. He would go back home and move on with his life as soon as this was over. She felt bad enough having him there night and day for the last two weeks. He put his entire life on hold just doing his job, following orders.

If Yates had not targeted her, he would have been home living his life. She would never have had the pleasure of meeting the breathtaking Agent Devon Walker, and she wouldn't be preparing to have her heart ripped from her chest when he finally left. It was pitiful. She knew she was falling in love with him. It should have been impossible to fall in love in two weeks, but somehow it was happening.

Devon cooked yet another scrumptious meal. Tonight, he made bacon-wrapped pesto pork tenderloin, jasmine rice, salad, and for dessert, white chocolate chip brownies with peanut butter swirls. Boy, this man could cook. She was going to hate takeout when he was gone. He was spoiling her with all these home-cooked meals. It was the healthiest she's eaten since she lived at home with her aunt and uncle. Their personal chef would prepare every meal, and every meal was healthy. Even the snacks in the fridge and pantry were healthy. Her aunt insisted on it.

"What are you thinking about, Mary?" he asked. "You look lost in thought."

"I was just wondering how much longer it could be until they apprehend Yates. You must be getting anxious to get back to your regular life. I know this can't be your idea of fun." She wondered if she looked as despondent as she sounded.

He reached his hand over and placed it on top of Mary's. "Sweetheart, there is no place I would rather be than right here with you," he said with a smile.

Instead of coming up with a nice, tender remark in return, she said, "Oh."

She quickly stood from the table and started collecting the dishes. She had a habit of turning into an embarrassed idiot any time he gave her the slightest compliment. Devon leaned back in his chair and enjoyed watching Mary get all flustered. Her cheeks turned red, and she was muttering to herself. He wondered if she even realized she did that when she was trying to work through something.

Something wicked sparked to life, and he found he wanted to see how red he could get her cheeks. If it was even possible, Devon thought Mary was even sexier when she was blushing. "Hey, Mary. Do you wanna play twenty questions?"

Surprised, she looked back at him. He had a weird look on his face. What was he up to? She raised an arched brow, skeptical as she asked, "what? Why?"

"Why? To give us something to do. I can skip watching Sports Center for one night. This'll let us get to know each other a little better. Didn't you ever play this game as a child? You have to answer the questions, so it's very intrusive."

"We have been stuck in the same apartment for two weeks. I think we know each other just fine." She sighed with furrowed brows.

It took everything in him not to laugh. Her cheeks were a deep scarlet, and if it was even possible, she was becoming more irritated. "Okay, then you won't mind playing?"

Determining she wouldn't be able to make it to her bedroom and lock the door before he caught up to her, she gave in to his little game. "Fine. But we can play while I do the dishes. I don't want to be up all-night cleaning the kitchen after we play your silly game."

"Sure." Moving towards the kitchen, he instinctively went to the wine fridge and pulled out a bottle of riesling. Over the past few weeks, he'd learned riesling was Mary's favorite, and so he had Matthews pick up a few bottles of a good vintage. Devon poured the wine into two glasses and set one on the counter next to Mary. He stepped over and jumped up to sit on top of the opposite counter next to her, his glass in hand. His feet dangled, and he looked carefree, like a little kid waiting to get a treat.

Mary picked up the glass of wine next to her hand and looked up at him, a question hiding in her gaze. "What's this for?"

Devon tried to look innocent. "What? We can't enjoy good wine?"

"You're up to something. I know for a fact that you prefer Lagavulin Scotch. I've not seen you drink anything else since we met. Matthews brings you a new bottle every time he brings us groceries. So, what's with the change?"

He lifted the glass to his lips and tipped it just enough that the wine barely touched the tip of his tongue. "I wanted something a little lighter tonight, and, damn, this is good."

His mischievous mood wasn't lost on her, but she tried her best not to let him see how turned on he made her with his little teases. He was in a rare mood indeed. She lifted the glass to her nose and found the fragrant aroma pleasantly surprising. "Fine. Thank you for the wine. Now let's start your silly game. The sooner we start, the sooner we can get this over with, and I can go to bed."

"Great. I'll go first," he said. He wanted to start her off slow. "Do you have any phobias?"

She placed another plate in the dishwasher, taking only a moment to think of her answer. "I absolutely love the water, but I'm terrified of dark water. The thought of not knowing what's beneath me when I'm in the water scares the hell out of me. And I don't just mean ocean water. My aunt and uncle used to take their boat up the Chesapeake, and far enough up the river, it turned into fresh water. So, nothing to worry about, right? Wrong.

"That's where I learned to water ski. One time, after I fell off my skis, I felt something brush my leg. I'll tell you what, I damn near walked on water until I got back onto the boat. I found out later that day that a fisherman caught a bull shark in that same area just a week earlier. Never before did I know a shark could survive in freshwater. The bull shark, apparently can, and that damn well could've been what brushed my leg. Ever since that day, I've been very anxious in water that's not crystal clear." She twisted her face in thought, scrunching her nose to focus. "Okay, my turn. Why did you pick the FBI?"

That one was easy. "Being an FBI agent runs in the family. My father, and his father before him, were all FBI agents. It would've shocked my parents if I'd chosen any other career. My parents told me that most of the games I played as a little kid revolved around the FBI. Instead of

83

cops and robbers, it was agents and robbers. I enjoy helping people and being the one to take bad guys off the street. An FBI agent is the only thing I've ever wanted to be. My turn," he said. "Out of all the careers you could have gone into, why forensic psychology?"

"As you can imagine, what happened to my parents really messed me up. For years, and I guess even today, I've been trying to figure out why it happened to them. Had they met Yates somewhere in their past, or just caught his attention on the street? And why did he do it? What makes any person have the desire to kill another human, let alone keep killing? Is it a sickness, a chemical imbalance? Do they just get a taste for it? I know what the textbooks say, but I don't always agree with them. My goodness, it's never ending. The authorities catch one psychopath, and two more sprout up. I just wish I could cut open their brains and learn all their secrets. Then, maybe, I'd be able to help the authorities stop it from happening again and again. Okay, me again." She wanted to change the subject before she became too emotional. "Why did you volunteer for this assignment?"

"What assignment?" He asked. He was too busy watching the play of emotions on Mary's face to concentrate on what she was saying.

"This one, watching me. Keeping me locked away... I mean safe."

"Actually, I didn't volunteer, I was *voluntold*. The chief ordered me to and there was nothing I could say to get out of it. And before you can get any crazy negative thoughts in that beautiful but stubborn head of yours, just know this: now that I'm here, I'm glad he made me do it, because it meant getting to know you. And the chief wanted the best agent for the duty, and he picked me. Because I'm the best."

"Conceited much?" She laughed. Without finishing the dishes, she refilled their glasses and moved toward the living room. If he was going to keep digging, she at least wanted to be comfortable through the ordeal.

"Okay, my turn again. If you could be anything in the world, what would it be?" He asked.

She took a moment to think about it. In the last few years, she had often battled with the option of changing her career field. After the terror she endured as a child, it was sometimes a torture in and of itself to study serial killers. "Um, I think I'd be a photographer. I've always loved to travel. My aunt and uncle tried to take me to a different country every year. I have so many photo albums of our travels. Most of the pictures are of the beaches in those countries, but I photograph what I love. Hopefully, someday soon, I'll be able to go back to some of those places. Now that I'm a little older, I feel I'd have a better appreciation for other cultures."

"I've never really traveled much. Maybe one day you can take me along and show me some of your favorite places. It would be an adventure."

There he was again, talking like they had a future together. This man was so confusing. What could it hurt to hope? It could hurt a whole awful lot to hope. "What about you? What would you be if you could be anything else but an agent?"

"That's easy. In the back of my mind, I always thought I'd be a pretty badass zookeeper."

"Really, a zookeeper? I can see it now, you in a polo shirt, those tight little tan shorts, and white socks that go up to your knees." She was laughing so hard tears ran down her cheeks.

"Yep. Like Steve Irwin. And I'd rock those shorts, by the way. One summer when I was little, my parents took my brother and me on a trip to different zoos and aquariums in the surrounding states. I remember being at one aquarium and we had to line up behind a roped off area because a zookeeper was about to walk the penguins through the halls. Being a little kid, I thought that was the most amazing thing in the world. I made my parents wait around the aquarium until it was time for the penguins to make the return trip through the halls and back to their enclosure.

"That memory always stayed with me. I even used to fantasize about dressing up like a big bad lion tamer, then following behind me would be these adorable little penguins. My brother used to make fun of me all the time, but I didn't care. That zookeeper looked like he had his dream job. He had a big smile on his face the whole time the penguins were on their march. Looking back at that day, I envy that zookeeper. I'm sure his job has its stresses, every job does, but waking up every day knowing you get to play with those adorable animals would make the hard days well worth it."

She didn't know what to say. Whatever she was expecting his answer to be, it surely wasn't that. His eyes showed a longing she'd never seen in him before. Devon's life would be so much different if he didn't follow in his father and grandfather's footsteps and had become that zookeeper that had caught the attention of a bright-eyed little boy.

He hadn't thought about those penguins for many years, and he suddenly had an urge to go to the aquarium. Maybe when this was all over, he'd take Mary and they could experience the penguins together. He didn't want to dwell on what could've been, so he rushed to the next question. "Me again. If money wasn't a factor, how would you want to spend the rest of your life?"

"Gosh, Devon, you're getting deep. But okay, I'll bite. If money wasn't a factor, I'd buy a tropical island. It would need to be big enough for my entire family and their families to live on. Like a homestead, but on an island. You already know I love the water, but the important thing about the island would be security. I'd want there to only be one way on and off the island. Maybe from the outside, it would look to be completely surrounded by an impenetrable rock wall, but there would be one secret entrance. You just wouldn't be able to find it unless you already knew about it. My family and I wouldn't need to worry about the horrors of the world. We would just be able to enjoy life. We could live without the drama of politics, social conformities, violence, public disturbance, and so much more. Just peace. I know it's naïve to think that I'd be able to go anywhere in this world and not be affected by its horrors, but I'd try my hardest not to let it affect my little part of the world. My paradise, my safe haven."

"And you said I was deep. I'd like to live on that secluded island with you. It sounds like paradise. Just being able to get away from the politics that shape how we're allowed to live our lives would be the ticket for me. You'd probably get bored pretty quick with your little island paradise, though. You appear to be a person who demands purpose. If you have everything handed to you, you'd lack that necessary purpose."

He was one hundred percent correct in his assumption. She did need purpose in her life, which is why she chose her career field. But damn, her little island paradise sounded tempting right about now. She decided to forget about what he just said, and dive back into their game. She'd never admit it to him, but she was rather enjoying his questions. "I have one that might amuse you. If you could star in a movie, what movie would it be?"

He couldn't help but chuckle. "That is a great question. I think I'd like to be in a horror movie, maybe something like Halloween."

"Really? Halloween? That's not really your normal shoot 'em up action movie."

"Yeah. Why not? I do have other tastes in movies besides action. There's so many, it's normally easy to find one playing on the TV. But I love horror movies. Well, slasher movies. I'm not such a big fan of pop-out and scare you movies like *Darkness Falls* or *Silent Hill*. Or movies with little kid ghosts, no thank you. And Michael Myers is a king in his movies. He can just walk as slow as he wants, and he still catches his target. And he can't die. There are how many now? Like a million Halloween movies? And Michael is still walking around killing people with a big ass knife. He's invincible."

It was refreshing to hear Devon talk like this. He gave her a warning look when she burst out laughing, but he said nothing in defense.

"My turn." He hesitated with his question, looking like he was debating asking it. "Why aren't you married?"

"Married? I guess I haven't found the right person yet. Don't get me wrong, I have dated, but men seem to get turned off when I tell them I pry into the minds of insane killers. Some of them have actually looked at me like I was the insane one. And that's all before they know about my blemished past.

"No one wants the drama that comes with someone like me. Someone that's been through having her parents murdered by a serial killer. I've tried everything from telling my date right away about my past to waiting until things got serious. No matter when I told them, it always got weird afterwards. Some of them acted okay with it right after I told them, but I ended up never hearing from them again. Although, I did date one guy that I later found out was only interested in me because of what happened to me. He was very mentally unstable. Last I heard, he was living in a padded cell somewhere. No matter what I do, my name will always be linked to *his* in the history books. Who in their right mind would want to be with someone like me?"

"I don't know why that'd deter men from committing to you. You don't hide your pain with drugs or alcohol. And you seem pretty grounded to me. It's their loss. Don't you dare give them another thought. Anyone that spends more than five minutes with you could see what an amazing person you are."

She was speechless. This man was so sweet. What was she going to do without him? "What about you? Why aren't you married?" She asked shyly.

"That's easy. The perfect woman hasn't come along yet."

"There's no such thing as the perfect woman, or man, for that matter. Perfect by definition is having no faults or imperfections. No human being is perfect. It's just not possible."

He smiled at her. "Oh yes, there is such a thing as the perfect woman."

"Okay then. If it's possible, what's your perfect woman like? I bet she has an amazing body." Realizing her glass was empty, and knowing she'd need more to continue with these questions, she moved from the sofa back into the kitchen.

"Of course she does. And she has blue eyes like sapphires, and brown hair, and legs that just won't quit." He stood up from the sofa and was moving closer to her with every sly description. "My perfect woman is insanely smart. I need to be with someone that can hold their own in a conversation. I can't tolerate a woman that can't hold a thought or think for themselves."

"Does she also have magic powers?"

They were standing face to face, and he was so close that their arms were touching, and if he shifted a little more, their faces would only be a breath away from each other.

"Are you mocking my perfect woman?" His lips pressed thin, but his eyes held humor. He was trying to act serious despite the threat of a grin, and stepped back slightly.

"Of course not. It's just hard to believe that she exists." She poured a glass of wine and took a long, dragging sip.

"My perfect woman will make me laugh but is also stubborn to a fault. So how does my perfect woman sound?"

Her breath caught in her throat. Was it a coincidence that a lot of the characteristics he described sounded like her? No. He was just messing around, right? She couldn't tell any more. Damn, the wine was going to her head. She needed to remember to stay clear minded around this man.

"Mary?"

She looked up at him. "Yes?"

"I asked you how my perfect woman sounds."

"She sounds amazing, and too good to be true."

"You know, when you meet the right person, they don't need to be perfect for everyone. They will be perfect for you."

What could she say to that? Everything this guy was saying was what she dreamed her whole life someone would say about her. But that was just a dream. "Go away and let me finish the dishes."

She heard him laughing as he walked away. Dishes would need to wait. She grabbed a bottle of wine out of the fridge and a glass and headed to her office. She needed to release some tension. Since the most obvious way to release tension was off the table, she'd throw herself into her work.

Devon watched her walk away. Man, he liked to mess with her. But he kind of wished she would have come and sat with him. He decided, after she had entertained him, to do something nice for her and finish the dishes.

Chapter 10

Mary woke up the next morning with a massive headache. She hadn't drank that much in years, but the night before was, to say the least, stressful. She needed release that she didn't have the privacy to achieve, and being in such close proximity to Devon made it worse. And, on top of that, just when she thought she was making a breakthrough with Yates, she wasn't. If only she could decipher how he chose his victims.

Her office looked like a tornado came through it, and that was completely out of character for her. There were papers taped to the walls, doors, and even the sides of her desk. The only untouched surface was the window. The natural light helped her think.

She needed a shower before she could face Devon. She could let the water wash away all her impure thoughts. While a hot shower did help, it didn't do as much as she had hoped. She pulled her hair into a messy bun, then threw on sweatpants and an oversized college t-shirt. It's not like she had any reason to get all dressed up. Right? After last night's round of questions, she was more confused about where they stood than she was before. She knew she found him attractive, but did he feel that same way about her? She was too much of a coward to ask. So, she'd continue her day as if nothing had happened.

When she walked out into the living room, Devon was nowhere to be seen. His partner Agent Matthews, however, was sitting on the couch watching the morning news. He looked completely relaxed with his feet propped on the coffee table with a large to-go coffee cup in one hand and the remote in another.

"Agent Matthews?"

Matthews turned and stood up. "Morning, Mary."

Looking around the living room, she asked, "Where's Devon?"

"Oh, he got a call early this morning. He forgot he had to take his yearly mandatory FBI physical fitness and weapons testing. He didn't want to wake you, so he had me run over and sit with you until he returned. I hope this is okay. I brought bagels and coffee; they're over on the kitchen table. Please help yourself. I didn't know what kind of bagels you liked, so I picked up a few of each flavor."

Disappointment dragged her lips into a heavy frown and she released a breath she'd held in too long. He'd left without saying goodbye.

"It'll be okay, Mary. He said he'd rush through his testing and be back before dinner. He really argued with the chief about delaying his testing. But of course, FBI standards win out. He also said you had a very long night and didn't want to disturb you." Matthews tried to suppress a smile. Devon told him all about the night before. Sometimes they gossiped like schoolgirls, and this was one of those times. Devon wanted advice on how to proceed with Mary, and Matthews wanted to make fun of his partner.

Mary relaxed a bit with his explanation. At least he wasn't running away after last night's conversation. She did have a very long night, and it was considerate of Devon to think about her comfort. It took her hours of tossing and turning before she succumbed to sleep. Now that she was a little more at ease, she was itching to get out of the apartment for a while. "I know this is a long shot, but do you think you could send Devon a message and see if he can get his dad to let us use his pool again? I'd really like to get out of the house today. And since we can only use the pool during school hours, I don't want to wait in case Devon is gone most of the day."

Matthews looked momentarily confused. "His dad's pool?" Then it clicked. "Oh yes, the one at his dad's school. Devon really wanted you to stay in today, since he wouldn't be here. Do you guys go swimming a lot?"

"No, not really. Swimming just helps me to think. We were just there yesterday, so maybe it's okay?"

After seeing the defeat on Mary's face, Matthews decided it wouldn't be a bad idea to get her out for some exercise, let her expend some of that pent-up energy. "Sure, why not? Let me send him a message. I'm sure that it will be okay."

Not five minutes later, Matthews received a text.

Devon: The school security guard can show you to the pool in the basement. I swear on everything you hold dear that if you bring her back with one hair out of place, I'll request a new partner and I'll pull strings to

make sure they partner you with Scott. I'll try to rush.

"Mary, we got the okay. Go grab your stuff. Walker said that if he can get done quick enough, he'd meet us over at the school. But Mary, Devon warned me you're going a little stir crazy waiting on the case to progress. Promise me this isn't a trick or anything to get out of the house and then run away from me?"

"Oh Matthews, you watch too many movies. I'd never do that to you. Devon? Possibly. But not you. I love life too much to make myself an unnecessary target." Excited, she rushed to her room, grabbed her gym bag, and they were out of the house in less than ten minutes.

He stood back in the crowd in front of the coffee shop, waiting to see if today was the day that an opportunity presented itself. He knew the one cop left very early this morning. Thinking that might have left Mary vulnerable, and he'd be able to make a move, he made his way over to her apartment. He wasn't able to get a camera inside the apartment, but he was able to install one in the hallway directly across from her door.

By the time he got to her apartment, another cop had shown up. Damn it. The cop had a hold of her arm, so he knew he wouldn't be able to separate the two. Today wouldn't be the day, but it was coming soon. They wouldn't be able to keep her behind closed doors forever. When they made the smallest slipup, that's when he'd strike. All of his plans were coming together. He just had to bide his time a while longer. He needed something to pass the time, though, and he knew just what he could do to amuse himself.

Chapter 11

Mary really pushed herself in the pool today. Pent up frustration can do that to a person. She was in the water for three hours when Matthews finally put a stop to it. He didn't have a swimsuit, and he didn't listen to her when she said it was okay for him to swim in his boxers, so he sat on the side of the pool with his feet dangling in the water. Even though his partner trusted him with his life, he knew Walker would kill him if he walked into the pool and Matthews was in his boxers within close proximity to Mary. Walker had admitted he had feelings for her, and he knew his partner well enough to know how unreasonably jealous he could become.

Mary only paused one time in those three hours, and that was to try to convince Matthews, once again, to come swimming with her.

"Matthews, I'm bored. Come swim with me." Mary called out from the middle of the pool.

Shaking his head, he said, laughing, "You really don't listen, do you? I already explained that I don't have a swimsuit, therefore there is no way I can get into the pool."

"And you, sir, didn't listen when I said you could swim in your boxers. What Devon doesn't know won't hurt him. I'm sure he's gone

96

swimming in his boxers before, so I don't see what the big deal is. You're covered."

"You don't see the big deal?" He groaned. "The big deal is that I would be in my underwear in your presence. Devon may be my partner and best friend, but he is also a very jealous and territorial man. And that man would not appreciate me joining you in the pool in anything less than proper swim attire. Do you understand?"

Tears ran down Mary's face as she tried her best to hold back her laughter. "No, Matthews, I don't understand a single word. Well, I do understand them, but I guess it's men I don't understand. Have it your way. I'm going to continue to enjoy this nice, refreshing water."

Mary was about to swim off when Matthews asked her something that'd been bothering him for a while. "Hey, Mary. Can I ask you a personal question? If you don't want to answer, that's okay. I won't be offended."

Pausing for a moment, a smile spreading over her face like the Cheshire Cat. "No, Matthews, I'm sorry, I won't sleep with you. I don't think Devon would like that very much. He is such a jealous, territorial man, you know."

Matthews thought his heart had stopped. This cheeky devil was playing with him. She definitely was a worthy opponent for Devon, and a smart match to his wit. He couldn't contain his smile. "No, Mary. I wouldn't be alive long enough to enjoy it. The question I had was, on that day we met you, at your school, why did you ask us to call you Mary and kind of snapped when we kept calling you miss?" He noticed her squeeze her eyes shut, as if she was in physical pain, and felt sorry for asking.

"It's not so much that you and Devon were calling me miss. It was how you were calling me miss. There's a reason they say to tone down bad news. When you give bad news, you are supposed to lower your voice and the rate of speaking. Usually, when you give good news, your tone raises, and the pace is faster, indicating excitement.

"When you and Devon called me miss that first day, it sounded like the way those police officers and shrinks spoke to me for the first few years after my parents' murder. I knew you were there with bad news, and it just brought so many emotions flooding back."

Trying to lighten the mood, Matthews asked, "but aren't you a shrink?"

Mary sucked in a dramatic gasp. "I most certainly am not. I am a forensic psychologist, not a *psychiatrist*. There are many areas of experience for a forensic psychologist, and mine are serial killers. Psychiatrists have those fancy couches in their offices for traumatized children to lie on while they dredge up the most painful experiences of their lives. I'm in no way putting down psychiatrists, they work wonders for many people. However, I've seen my fair share, and I don't think I ever want to go back."

Mary didn't want to say anything more on the subject. Digging up the past was the last thing she wanted to do in the pool. She turned, dove under the water, and didn't stop again until Matthews told her it was time to go.

The ride to and from the gym was the same as if Devon was the one escorting her. Matthews went through the motions, checking the hallways, cars, and even the women's locker room. It was different, though, less personable than if Devon was with her. Maybe he was just embarrassed about asking her that question about the day they met. He'd apologized about a hundred times since they'd left the pool.

The mood lightened when they arrived back at her apartment. She looked up at the stairs and groaned as she rubbed her lower back, considering taking the elevator, which she never did unless she was bringing in something heavy.

"You're walking a little stiff, Mary. Do you want me to carry you up the stairs? It wouldn't be any trouble at all, I promise." He said cheerfully.

"Oh, I'm sure you'd love that. Now, thank you. I'll make it just fine. You can go right ahead if it bothers you that I'll slow you down. Or you can just keep your mouth shut and carry my bag." She tossed the bag at his head, which wasn't very fast, and started up the stairs, pulling on the railing with each step for support.

As soon as Matthews made sure the apartment was secure, Mary made a beeline for her bathroom, craving a hot shower. Dropping her wet towel and gym bag inside her bedroom door, she didn't even have the energy to put anything away before she did something about her screaming muscles. She pushed herself too far, and now she was paying for it. It was exactly what she needed, though.

Succumbing to the ache in her muscle, untouched by the heat of the shower, she sat down in the bottom of the tub and tried to relax. A sudden swell of emotions came over her as she sat there with her head back and eyes shut beneath the streaming water. Sorrow for her parents, grief for Yates's other victims, heartache for her aunt and uncle who put their lives on hold to raise her, and panic for Devon consumed her. She didn't know how long she had been crying when she heard a knock on her door. She knew it was Devon, just by his knock. He knocked every time before entering her office when she was working. This was one time she wished he'd just go away.

"Mary, are you okay?" He called through the door. "I wanted to tell you dinner was almost ready, but then I heard you crying." When she didn't answer him, he came in. He could see through the shower door that she was sitting on the floor. He knelt down, bringing himself level with her. "Mary, darling, talk to me. What's wrong?" He could see her head come up. He knew a foolproof way to get her to come out. "If you don't come out and talk to me, I'm going to come in there with you."

She didn't immediately respond, so he stood up and took his suit jack off. That did the trick. He saw her start to stand up. Knowing that Devon didn't make threats, and he'd have come into the shower, she knew she'd have to get out and talk to him. "If you leave the room, I can get out of the shower. I can be out in five minutes."

"Are you sure? If you need help washing your back, I believe I'm more than qualified to help."

"Devon." She said with so much exasperation he could hear it in her voice from outside the shower.

"Okay, five minutes, then I come in." He said as he left the bathroom.

She came into her bedroom about ten minutes later, still looking flushed. Was it from the hot water or her being upset? Devon was sitting, waiting, on her bed when she came out of the bathroom in a long t-shirt and shorts. He gently tapped the bed next to him as an invitation to come sit next to him. He was determined to find out what had upset her. Matthews said nothing noteworthy happened while they were out. He wouldn't lie to Devon, so Mary must have been upset about something else.

Without hesitation, Mary padded over to the bed, looked at Devon, sighed, and then sat down. All she hoped for was to not get another one of his lectures. She wasn't in the mood for it. "How was your training today?" She asked, trying to change the subject before he started.

"I did great, of course, because I'm awesome. Now stop trying to distract me. Will you please tell me why you're upset?"

She shook her head. Maybe if she kept dodging the question, he'd give up on digging. Not likely, though, but she'd try, anyway. "What makes you think I'm upset?"

That was ridiculous. It was clear as day, by nothing more than the look on her face, she was upset. "Mary, did something happen today? If Matthews lied about today being uneventful, I may go whoop his ass. He told me you guys went swimming and nothing else. He did, however, admit you tried to get him to swim in his boxers. For which he smartly declined, and we'll talk about that later, sweetheart. You need to know something right now. As Matthew already told you, I'm an insanely jealous person."

She giggled, despite herself. "No, nothing happened besides us going swimming. You know swimming relaxes me, and it was nice of him to take me. Thank you for calling your dad. I know you were busy. Just so you know, there would've been nothing wrong with him swimming in his boxers. It would have just been swimming. And why would you be jealous, Devon? Hmmm?"

"Nevermind, we'll talk about it later. I know I've told you before, and I'll tell you again: I'll do anything for you, Mary. But I still want to know why you're upset. Swimming doesn't make you cry. If anything, swimming puts you in a better mood. So, what's going on? I won't let you have any of my famous chicken parmesan until you talk to me. And believe me, you don't want to miss my chicken parmesan."

Her stomach betrayed her by growling so loud they both heard it. "Fine," she grumbled. "I'm only giving in because I don't want to starve." She took a deep breath. "I'm upset about Yates. I'm upset with all the horror that man has caused to so many people. And the children. Oh God, Devon, the children. Yes, it's horrific what he does to parents, but does he also need to take the lives of the children? They can't defend themselves. They're completely innocent, and he takes that innocence before they even have a chance to make their place in this cruel and evil world. It's not fair. I've tried, and tried, to understand what makes this guy tick, but it's impossible. I have dissected the minds of Jeffery Dahmer, John Wayne Gacy, Ted Bundy, and many more. But I can't seem to understand Jimmy Yates. It's like my mind goes blank and I can't remember any of my training as soon as that man's name comes to mind. I just can't focus. It's so frustrating. I want this bastard behind bars, or preferably in the ground, so he can't hurt anyone else ever again."

She put her head in her hands and cried again. Devon pulled her to his side and up onto his lap. "Do you think maybe you have a block because you are actually part of his story? That it's because you have a personal stake in this specific killer?"

"Why do you need to sound so logical?" She asked without raising her head. "I just wish I was able to help the authorities more by giving them the information about how he chooses his victims. Maybe then I can help stop more murders. Maybe I'd finally get the answers I've been searching for my entire life. Why my family? What made him target my parents? I need to know."

"Even if we're unable to catch Yates before he kills again, in no way is it your responsibility to be the one to stop him. We're working with many other agencies to get ahead of him. He's evaded the police for years, but now that they know what he wants, they'll work tirelessly to catch him. It's not your job to catch him, but we'll gladly take any information you have on him that could help expedite the process. Even if you can't provide us with any information, like I said, it's not your job, so you have nothing to feel responsible about. Okay? Your only job right now is to listen to me so I can keep you safe."

"What does he want?" She asked succinctly.

He was afraid that she'd caught that. He didn't even mean to say it, it just slipped out. "You, Mary. He wants you. I swear to you, nothing is going to happen to you. Will you please believe me?"

She slowly nodded her head. "What about you?"

"What about me?"

"You're the one I worry about, not myself. I don't know what I'd do if you got hurt trying to protect me. I don't want anyone to get hurt because this psycho feels like he has some sort of vendetta against me. Sure, I've always known there was a chance I'd die at the hand of that murderous psychopath, but I've accepted that. What I can't accept is if something would happen to you." She tried to hold back a sob but failed.

He reached up and placed a hand on her shoulder. "Mary, listen. You knew when we first met that I'm an FBI agent. It comes with the job. They could be placed in dangerous situations at any time. I fully understand and accept that aspect of my job and I'm not worried. We train for situations just like this. We're prepared to defend ourselves and prepared to be confronted by an aggressive attacker. The FBI makes sure we know how to handle ourselves before we're allowed into the field. It's my job to keep you safe, not the other way around, but you know what?"

"No, what?"

"I'd protect you even if I wasn't an agent. You are special, Mary. You don't seem to realize that yet. But if you let me, I'll show you. So, what do you say? Will you give me the time to show you what I see when I look at you?"

Her heart fluttered with excitement while fighting off a rising sense of doubt. She wasn't used to allowing her life decisions to be determined by someone else, and that included her safety. "I'll try, Devon." She wanted to change the subject. "So, are you going to feed me now, or am I actually going to starve?"

He let out a booming laugh. "Fine, but you better talk up my food. Matthews has never had it. I don't cook for just anyone. So that should prove how special you really are. He's probably wondering if we disappeared, so we've better get out there. I left him to make the salad, with a lot of grumbling on his part. He's great with a gun, but his chopping skills need some work. When I left him, he was butchering the cucumbers. Try not to say anything, though. I don't want to offend him about his cucumbers when he was just trying to help. I'll find something else to make fun of him for later. Will you do me a favor?"

"Of course." She was trying not to laugh over the fact Devon was trying to protect another grown man's feelings about destroying a vegetable.

"As much as I love to see you walking around in those tiny shorts, I don't want to have to gouge my partner's eyes out if he so much as looks at your legs. Would you please put on some pants? As soon as he leaves, feel free to put your shorts back on, or not. I'll leave that decision up to you."

She could see the twinkle in his eyes. He was getting jealous again, and that made her smile. "Of course, I'll put pants on. Let me finish getting ready and I'll be there in five." She reached up quickly to grab his hand when he moved to walk out the door. "Thank you, Devon, for making me feel better."

He leaned over and gave her a kiss on the top of the head. "Anything for you, darling."

Chapter 12

Dinner went better than she could've even imagined. It was nice to have Matthews there with them, and it was more entertaining listening to him enjoy the meal. He groaned with almost every bite. It was hard not to laugh, but she didn't want to hurt his feelings. "Oh. My. Gosh. Walker, where'd you learn to cook, man? This is amazing. Can I hire you to be my personal chef? I can't believe we've been partners all these years, and you never cooked for me. Never even brought me in some leftovers. That's mighty selfish of you. I think that if you don't start providing me with food, I'll have to request another partner." Mary couldn't hold in the laughter a moment more, and Matthews turned and winked at her.

Devon let out a booming laugh. It had become one of her favorite sounds. "You couldn't afford me. My grandmother taught me to cook, so she confided many family secrets to me. She never had any granddaughters, so she dragged me into the kitchen every chance she could. Apparently, I took to cooking very quickly, and if I do say so myself, I'm damn good at it. Those are some of the best memories I have of my grandmother, and I still use her recipes today. The sauce on the pasta is her recipe, and I'll never make it any other way. A girl I was dating once told me my pasta sauce tasted like Prego. Needless to say, we broke up that night." Laughter echoed around the table.

Dinner seemed to go on for hours. The conversation flowed as easily as the drinks. As much as Devon and Mary enjoyed each other's company, it was nice to see Matthews and get some information about the outside world. Over the past weeks, they'd kept the news off as much as possible. The media always twisted stories for their own agendas, and neither Mary nor Devon wanted anything but the facts. She overheard Devon tell Matthews not to bring up Yates at dinner, that he wanted her to have one night being carefree. It was very thoughtful of Devon to be so concerned about her feelings.

After dinner was done, Mary shooed them out of the kitchen and insisted on cleaning up. Matthews argued at first, but then conceded. The men grabbed their drinks and moved to the balcony. Devon's nighttime routine included surveying the surrounding area. From her balcony, he could see for a few blocks. He'd always try to pick out new people, new vehicles, and anything that looked suspicious. Tonight was no different. He glanced around the street below, watching people go about their business. The only thing different tonight were a few new vehicles.

He quickly pulled out his phone, activated the camera, and zoomed in to take pictures of the license plates. He'd email them to the office to check them out. Normally, he sent all his information to Matthews to verify, but Matthews was standing right next to him. He didn't want to have to wait for him to get back to the office to check the plates. Devon pocketed his phone and turned to finish his conversation with his partner.

About twenty minutes later, both Devon's and Matthew's phones buzzed. The agent on duty informed them that the black panel van on the street came up as stolen. Not wanting to alarm Mary, Matthews decided he'd check it out. The trouble was getting him out without making Mary suspicious.

Matthews walked over to Mary and gave her a big hug. "Thanks for letting me crash the party tonight, Mary. That was a great meal and even better company. We'll need to do it again sometime soon. I still can't believe Walker's never cooked for me before. Some partner."

Mary smiled. He sounded like a sad little boy being sent to his room without dinner. "Matthews? Oh, my goodness. You must think I'm so rude. I've never even asked your first name. I'm so sorry."

He pulled her in for another hug just to annoy his partner. It was obvious how jealous Walker became when he gave Mary the first hug. They could hear his huffing and sulking from across the room, but both Mary and Matthews ignored his childish behavior. "It's Michael. Mary, I don't think you have it in you to be rude. I don't mind being called Matthews."

"You can let go of her now, Matthews. You've shown your appreciation," Devon announced as he crossed to where they were standing.

She ignored his blatantly jealous remark. "Thank you for being so kind, Michael. It was such a pleasure to have you over tonight. In the future, I'll have Devon make extra food when he cooks, so I can send some leftovers home with you. Also, how about at least every time you bring groceries you stay for dinner? That doesn't mean you need to bring us something to stop by for dinner or a visit. You are always welcome in my home."

He lit up with humbled gratitude. "Sounds like a plan." He turned to Devon as he leaned on the counter at the other end of the kitchen. "I'll check in later. Let me know if you need anything." Devon nodded, "later man, stay safe."

Matthews's smile didn't waver as he moved towards the door, determined not to show the slightest hint of something wrong. He'd go check out the van and assess the situation. Hopefully, it was nothing to worry about, and was just a coincidence that someone parked the stolen van on this street. There were a bunch of industrial buildings within walking distance, so that could be the case. But he had a rule not to believe in coincidences.

The shadows of the neighboring buildings provided the necessary concealment Matthews needed to move closer to the van without being seen. Reaching into his jacket pocket, he pulled out the latex gloves he always carried with him. Creeping next to but not touching the van, he peered into the dark window. As far as he could tell, after a quick inspection, he couldn't see any shadows pass the windows, so it was safe to assume no one was inside. What he found on the passenger side seat was questionable and disturbing.

Hastily thrown on the seat were a pair of high-powered binoculars and rubber gloves. Those were not things normally stored in a vehicle, even a stolen one. While there was no proof it was Yates, if it was, he didn't want to let him know they were onto him by disturbing anything in the van. He called the MPD to have them send a unit out and a tow truck. Since the van came back as registered as stolen, it wouldn't be uncommon for it to be towed. Then they could take it back to their precinct and try to get some prints. He sent Devon a quick text.

Matthews: *Binoculars and gloves are visible. Watch your back. I'll call to-morrow with more info.*

Devon: *Got it.*

Devon replied as he wandered towards the couch to lie down. He pivoted in step and moved to the balcony to give one more look around the neighborhood. Although unnecessary, he'd wait and watch the van until the authorities arrived to secure the vehicle. If this was Yates, he wouldn't let any evidence they might pull from the vehicle become compromised. "Yates, you bastard, you can try to hide, but we'll find you. You're not as smart as you think you are. When you make one tiny mistake, we'll finally have you, and this time, you won't slip away."

Mary had already gone to bed, so he didn't need to worry about hiding the rage he was feeling inside. Fresh fear reared up within him. If the vehicle did, in fact, belong to Yates, that meant he might have been close for a while. If that were the case, how much longer would he be able to keep Mary safe? He'd done all he could for the night. There wasn't much he'd be able to do until they had more information. After the tow-truck left with the van, he made another pass around the apartment, checking the doors and windows, making sure every lock was secure and there were no signs of tampering. He was extra cautious with his checks after the apartment was vacant for a few hours. Since Mary and Matthews were gone this afternoon, once Devon arrived back at the apartment, he double checked every nook and cranny. Nothing was getting into this apartment without him knowing about it. That he was sure about. He needed to get some sleep, though. Things might ramp up and he'd need to be on his A-game. Catching Yates and putting him behind bars was the goal, but the thought of leaving Mary filled him with uneasiness.

Jimmy leaned against the alley wall, looking up at Mary's apartment. That cop was once again out scouting. He noticed two of them eyeing his van, so he had plenty of time to move locations. He suppressed his thrill of excitement when the other cop walked right past him. They think they're so smart, but he just proved them wrong. He could've taken that one out right there, but killing a cop would make them put Mary into more of a lockdown, and then it'd be harder to get to her. No, he had to let them think they're smarter than him, then he'd attack. He'd go after the two interfering bastards after he had his hands on Mary. He'd go after them just for causing him frustrations.

He retreated further into the alley as a local police car glided by. Son of a bitch, he'd need to find new wheels. At least he anticipated something like this, and he already removed most of his belongings. He leaned over and rifled through his duffel bag to pull out his newest batch of pictures. The pictures were mostly the same: Mary tucked safely away in her apartment while the cop assessed the neighborhood. He only had a few from the camera posted across from her door. But he was able to catch glimpses inside every time the door opened.

They really were getting cozy together, but they'd soon let their guards down. He caught one photo of Mary in a tank top and a pair of short shorts. She wasn't the little goody two shoes she made people believe she was. Yates knew the truth. She was a whore, just like her mother. He tried to calm himself down. He'd give them a little more time to become complacent, and then he'd strike. They'd never see him coming.

Chapter 13

Over the next two weeks, Mary and Devon fell into a peaceful routine. He opened doors for her, pulled out her chair, and focused on the
little things. When she would fall asleep on the couch while they
watched movies, he would cover her with a blanket and move her head
to his lap, where she'd be more comfortable. A few times, she woke up
and found he was sound asleep. He couldn't be comfortable sleeping
sitting up, but he always made sure she was comfortable.

Mary made time to watch Sports Center at night, even though she
never understood the desire men had to watch sports highlights after
they'd spent hours watching the actual game. Just sitting next to him on
the couch, close enough that their arms and legs were touching, was
what made her come and join him night after night even though she was
completely, and utterly, bored. Since she didn't really care for sports,
she sat with a magazine or book and read. She loved watching his face
change with the game. He was so animated while watching TV. It was
mesmerizing. He was upset any time one of his favorite teams would
make a bad move, and argue senselessly with the screen if a referee
made a bad call. There were times he jumped up and down on the sofa
when that happened.

With his job, he needed to be serious all the time, and that meant not letting people know what he was thinking. When he first started this detail, Mary had no idea what he was on his mind, and she often thought he looked irritated. Lately, though, he was opening up and letting his guard down around her, and that gave her hope. It felt like the beginning of a relationship.

Even so, she knew nothing could happen while she was technically his assignment, but maybe something more could happen after. It never hurts to hope. After a month together, they learned so much about each other, good and bad. She had a crazy past, but he knew that, because it was the reason for his assignment. Would he ever consider a relationship with someone with so much baggage? They would need to see where things went on their own. Mary knew one thing, though. She had never felt this way about anyone, ever, and it scared her.

She blocked out those thoughts and refocused on the time they had together. Turning her attention back to her magazine as her eyes drooped, tired from a long day of research, she shivered. It was getting chilly in the apartment, and Devon grabbed the afghan from the back of the sofa and wrapped it around her. Pulling her to his side, she shifted until she was leaning onto his lap. Comfortable there, she nodded off. A terrible mistake as the game was coming down to the wire.

On more than one occasion, Devon jumped and yelled at the TV, forgetting something was in his lap. Normally it was a plate, or bowl, but this time, it was Mary. She hadn't been asleep long when the buzzer sounded and the whistle blew. And the referee made a stupid call, a foul for unsportsmanlike conduct. And with that, Devon, infuriated, jumped up and Mary flew to the floor.

It took her a moment to realize what happened, but as soon as clarity came back, she pressed her lips together to suppress her laughter. Devon looked so crestfallen, and with fear in his eyes.

Hands flying to the side of his head, he's momentarily frozen in place by his careless actions. "Oh Mary, I'm so sorry. I'm so stupid. I don't know how I forgot you were laying there. Here, let me check you out. Are you okay? Nothing hurt or broken? Do you need to go to the hospital?" He knelt down next to her.

She laughed and grabbed his hands to get him to stop rambling from worry and see that she's okay. "Devon! Look, I'm fine. I took worse falls than this when I'd ride horses at my uncle's Pennsylvania estate. I loved riding the wild, untamed horses before the trainers broke them, and they didn't care if they threw you. Sometimes I felt like it was a game with them. I fell on the floor, that's all."

He looked at her like she lost her mind. He reached up and started rubbing his forehead like he was trying to fight off a headache. "Are you sure you're okay?"

"Yes." She sighed, gently cupping his cheek. "I'm fine. Now will you please calm down? I'm going to go to bed. Are you going to be okay?"

"Me? You're the one that I catapulted onto the floor." He stopped when he heard her chuckle. "Fine. I'll take your word for it. But I'll make it up to you. Tomorrow I'm going to bake you a cake."

He always tried to make up for anything with food. She figured out early on that cooking and baking were like a safety net for him. It took him back to a happy place. A place where he could hide momentarily from the real world.

"A cake sounds amazing. Good night, Devon." Mary said as she stood up and headed down the hall towards her room, realizing how much in that moment she wanted to stay in the living room with him, but decided some distance to think about her feelings was best.

He sank back down on the sofa and turned off the TV, sports were ruined for the night. "Good night, Mary. Sweet dreams."

Chapter 14

Devon was getting out of the shower when his phone rang. He checked the time. It was seven in the morning. As soon as he read the name on the screen, he contemplated not answering the call. But he knew the chief would keep calling and calling until he answered. He also knew if he didn't answer his phone, the chief would call the house phone, and Devon didn't want Mary disturbed.

"Agent Walker," Chief Parker said, sounding unusually rattled, "I need you to get Ms. Anderson ready to leave her apartment. She's going to be picked up in twenty minutes by private security provided by the congressman. Before you say a word, I don't want any arguments from you. This is an order, not a request."

In an instant, dread washed over Devon and he felt sick to his stomach. The chief wouldn't move Mary unless something was popping off, and that made him nervous. Especially since he was being ordered to hand Mary off to unknown security officers and not the FBI. No, he was the only one that could make sure Mary stayed protected. "Wait. What? For the last month, I've only left her side twice, once on your orders, and once for personal reasons. Your number one priority was to keep

Mary under lock and key with me as her babysitter, remember? What's changed? Why now?"

Chief Parker sighed so loud into the phone Devon knew instantly the situation was bad. "Yates is the reason for the sudden change, Walker. He struck again, murdered a well-known family in town, loved by the community. The media's going to run with this, and Mary is going to be front and center. I need your eyes at the latest crime scene. You're my best agent, and with all the time you've spent with Ms. Anderson, maybe you'll have some new insights. We need to catch him, and fast. He may target Mary sooner than we thought."

"If she's going to be a target, then I need to stay with her. Or get her out of the city. I'm sure I can make up a good enough excuse to whisk her away. What if we get her aunt to suggest some time away from D.C.? From what Mary's told me, she'll do anything for her aunt. What if–"

"I said no," the chief snapped. "Now do as you're told and get ready to hand her off. Then get over here right away." He hung up before Devon could say another word.

Emotions and information swirled around his brain. Quickly trying to analyze every moment of every day, he's been with her for the last four weeks. Trying to justify this nagging feeling of dread at the mention of leaving her. Her safety was his responsibility, and he didn't trust anyone else with her, except for Matthews. However, he was still an FBI agent and had to follow orders, but that didn't mean he liked it. This was the first lead they had on Yates since his message at the University. Now he had to go prepare Mary for the news. If there was any way for him to keep her in the dark, he'd do it. But he knew she'd pick up on the change

117

in their routine right away. She'd catch on and know something was wrong.

Anytime they talk about Yates, she'd say they needed to catch him before he hurts anyone else. She felt it was her fault he was back in the area. It wasn't, but it was hard to convince that woman of anything. She was stubborn to the core. And he loved that trait. Right now, her stubborn streak was pinpoint focused on Yates. She wouldn't take the news that he killed another family well at all. She became more withdrawn at any mention of his child victims. If Devon thought he'd be able to keep this new information about the family from her, he would. But as soon as he mentioned Yates, she'd know. He'd order her new security officers to limit the radio or TV exposure to keep the specific details from her. She was already going to be devastated enough, so no reason to add more to it.

When he walked into the kitchen, Mary was leaning over the stove. Dear lord, she looked amazing in her old, knee-length, oversized shirt. As she leaned over, the shirt rode up so high in the back he could see the perfect curve of her behind. She had no shorts underneath and for a moment he forgot what it was he'd come in for. What was wrong with him? A family was just murdered, and he was here wondering what Mary would look like without her shirt on.

She hadn't heard him approach. When she turned around, she screamed and dropped her spatula. He was closer than expected and he hadn't realized she had headphones in. If he had, he would have called out to her. She'd been extra jumpy lately. Later, he'd need to figure out why. Maybe she found out something about Yates that had her on edge. No, that couldn't be it. She'd tell him if she found something that could help the FBI. It must be something else. Tonight, when they got back to the apartment, he'd cook her a nice dinner, and he'd get her to tell him what's on her mind.

He reached out and pulled her into a hug. "Gosh, I'm so sorry. I thought you heard me approaching."

She laughed. "Of course I didn't hear you. You walk around like you float on air. You never make a sound unless you want to. Sometimes I look at your feet to see if you're levitating."

He knew she was just joking. She joked when she was nervous or frightened. "Why don't you plate up your breakfast and come to the table? We need to talk."

"Hmm. Do you mean talk or talk-talk?" She looked at him with uncertainty. Something had him disturbed.

"It's nothing bad. You're such a pessimist."

"I think I have earned the right to be a pessimist."

"True." He waited until she had at least some of her breakfast down before giving her the bad news. Looking at his watch, he said, "In about fifteen minutes, some security people your uncle hired will be here to pick you up."

Her hands began shaking so hard, she dropped her fork. That was okay, because her hunger was instantly gone.

Noticing how pale she'd become, and the sweat that now covered her brow, he hoped to elevate some of her distress. "Now before you go getting crazy thoughts in your head, the chief just needs my expertise on a case, then I'll pick you back up and we can continue being stuck with each other. Hopefully, I'll get it wrapped up before dinner."

Even after he explained the situation, she still looked upset. Her eyes were glistening with tears threatening to spill onto her cheeks. "I know you've never asked for this detail, and you've been stuck here with me for weeks, so if you need a break, I can go stay with my aunt and uncle. Their home is like a fortress. Yates could never get me there. I don't want to be a burden, I've never wanted to be a bother to anyone. Especially not you."

He got out of his chair, walked around the table, and pulled her seat back. He lowered to his knees in front of her and grabbed her hands. "Now listen to me and listen well. These last few weeks have been very enjoyable for me. Yes, I'll admit at first, I thought this was going to be a punishment when I got this assignment, but over the past weeks, I've come to know what a great woman you are. We've had great conversations, and we have fun just sitting around the house. Most people who get stuck together for as long as we've been usually start to get on each other's nerves. Climbing up the walls for a moment of privacy, but not us. We are so comfortable with each other that we can just be ourselves.

"The only reason you're going to be picked up is that I can't disobey orders and the chief really does need my help. Hopefully, I'll be able to pick you up later this afternoon. Okay? Believe me, if he didn't need my help, you wouldn't be getting rid of me. I know I'm stepping over a line here, but I enjoy spending time with you, and not just because my job forces me to. You're a great woman, and hopefully once Yates is behind bars, we can continue to spend time together. No matter what happens, we are always going to be in each other's lives. I won't let you go. So, let's get through today and we can talk more tonight. Okay?"

Beaming with joy as he rose from the floor, she leapt up and threw her arms around him in a tight embrace. "Of course, I'll still want to see you. I thought maybe you were getting sick of me."

Mary hadn't smiled like this in the last few days, and she deserved to be happy. His heart fluttered, sharing in her joy and thrilled he could bring a smile back to her face. Hopefully she'd still be able to smile at him after she realizes he didn't tell her the whole truth about where he was going. He didn't technically lie, but he didn't tell the truth either. He pulled away. "Now, as much as I love to see you in that old shirt, I don't want anyone else seeing you in it. Why don't you go change and get ready? I'll clean up breakfast. Your new security detail should be here any time."

A mischievous grin spread across her face. "So, you like my shirt, huh? I'll need to remember that," she said as she went into her room and softly closed the door.

Minutes later, as Mary walked out of her room, Devon opened the door to let in the security team. Maybe 'let in' weren't the right words. Devon had them cornered in the entryway, giving them the third degree while taking photos of their identification. He turned when he heard her in the hall and held up a finger, then pointed to the two guards. She knew better than to argue with him or point out he was being rude to her uncle's employees.

"You two don't move." He stated to the guards. He quickly punched the speed dial on his phone. "Hey Matthews, I just emailed you some photos. Can you check out the two IDs and get back to me right away?" He listened for a moment then said, "yes, I know the chief is waiting on me and I don't care, he can keep waiting until I make sure the people that are going to be guarding Mary are legit. So, hurry, won't you?"

About five minutes later, Devon's phone dinged with a message. "Okay guys, you're okay to take Mary." He pulled two cards from his wallet. "If there's any change in your itinerary, you need to call me before you move. Got it? "

The guards huffed as they returned their IDs and his card to their wallets. Their employer warned them he'd be difficult, but this was overboard. Did he know the rigorous background check they had to go through to get their current positions? And now this guy was giving them orders.

It made Mary feel good to see Devon was still taking her safety so seriously. At least one of them was, after a month and no one word from Yates, she had her doubts he didn't just move on. If anything, she felt like a burden. No matter how many times Devon assured her that wasn't the case, it was still hard to believe.

Mary grabbed her purse when Devon stepped in front of her. "Now, I need you to listen. Okay?" She nodded, trying not to smile.

He liked to give her lectures on being safe. He did it even when she went out to the balcony to have her morning coffee and get some fresh air. Because of Devon, she knew all the likely places around her apartment that someone could lie in wait to attack. She also knew to check the surrounding apartments' roof tops for possible sniper activity. She was much happier when she was oblivious to almost everything around her.

He was snapping his fingers in front of her face. "I mean it, Mary. Focus. This is important. These are the security guards your uncle hired to keep you safe while I work this case. Hopefully, I'll be able to pick you up in a few hours, but if not, I need you to listen to them. I know you don't like to take orders, but they have your safety in mind. Maybe it'll help to remember they're employed by your uncle. So, before you fight them on every decision, just remember they report to him and follow his orders, and mine, of course. Yates is unpredictable, so we need to be careful. Just go to your uncle's house and kick back and relax. Maybe spend the day relaxing by the pool with your aunt. Okay? Have some girl time."

She gave him a mock salute. "Yes, Sir."

He glared at her. "I mean it, smarty pants. You need to be careful. Okay? I couldn't take it if anything happened to you. Tonight, when I pick you up, I think we need to have a little talk. A talk-talk."

Her heart raced, and she felt hopeful. She really cared for Devon, and she knew he cared for her. Maybe tonight they'd move forward in their relationship. She slowly nodded. "You'll be careful too, right? I know you can't tell me where you're going, or about the case, but be safe, okay?"

He affectionately cupped her face in his hand. "Of course, I'll be safe. We have a rematch in scrabble to complete. I still think you cheated."

She let out a full-hearted laugh. "Just because you didn't believe me xertz was a real word and had to look it up, that doesn't constitute cheating."

They all turned to walk out the door. Just like with Devon, the two guards wouldn't let her go anywhere first. Once they got to the parking lot, Devon checked out the car, even though he'd watched the guard do the same. She knew the guards would be glad to get rid of Devon. He had a special talent for rubbing people the wrong way, but that's what made him a great agent. He never took anything for granted.

As he closed the car door for Mary, Devon had a bad feeling again. Yates could be out there watching them, and he'd know Mary was on the move. He just needs to meet the chief at the latest crime scene, give him his advice, then get back to Mary. The chief said something about the latest victims would cause a media frenzy around Mary. Devon needed to find out the details. Without being at the crime scene, he couldn't think how this murder could tie back to Mary, except through the connection to Yates.

He wanted the day to be over with and to pick Mary up from her uncle's house by dinner time like he told her he would. He'd feel better once they returned to her apartment, where he could ensure they were secure and she was safe. She was his responsibility. If anything happened to her, he'd burn D.C. to the ground to find Yates.

After she was gone with her uncle's security, it took him about thirty minutes to reach the latest crime scene. Morning traffic was a bitch, and the vehicle he was driving didn't have lights or sirens. When he pulled up, the place was swarming with so many people; it looked like the whole bureau was there, plus the MPD. Something was off. Devon spotted Matthews leaning against his car with his head in his hands. He knew that blood and carnage didn't bother Matthews, so something was definitely wrong. Matthews was a Marine and had seen terrible things in Afghanistan. Nothing normally fazed him. How could a crime scene make him tremble and grind the heels of his hands into his eyes as if to scrub away what he saw? Then it dawned on him. *Children.* If this was truly a Yates crime scene, there would be children inside.

As soon as he walked through the door, he knew he was correct about the reason for Matthews's behavior. Devon had seen photos from Yates's earlier crime scenes, but it was completely different in person. In all his years in the bureau, he'd never seen anything like this. The whole family, dad, mom, son, daughter, and even the dog, were in the living room. Their bodies laid in a circle, staged for them to be found.

The horrible part was that all of them had their faces sliced and peeled off their skulls. Yes, he knew that was Yates's signature, but to see it in person was different.

Until that moment, he never thought about Mary finding her parents with their faces removed. Oh God, what she had to have gone through as a child nearly broke his heart. The only saving grace was that she didn't seem to remember the details of finding them. Hopefully, that part of her torment would always stay repressed, and she'd remember them as they were before Yates butchered them. After seeing the bloody scene, if it was at all possible, Devon felt Yates was even more of a monster than he originally believed.

Devon walked through the living room and found the chief. He and a few officers were outside of what he assumed was the door to a study or office. The chief was irate and shook his finger at Agent Scott. Cutting off his tirade mid sentence, he drew his attention from Scott as he noticed Devon standing just over Scott's shoulder. Pushing Scott aside, he now started shouting at Devon. "Agent Walker, finally, you're here. It took you long enough. Is Ms. Anderson safe with her other security?"

"Yes, Sir. I even sent a copy of their IDs to Matthews, and he verified them for me. That's the reason for my delay."

"Good. Good. You did always know how to do your job. However, I want you to call them back and tell them we are sending over some more guys right now. They're already on their way and should be there soon. I want them aware of the added security. She needs more protection than the two guards. I even have an agent calling the congressman now. I never should've insisted you head over here and put Ms. Anderson in the custody of anyone else. She needs absolutely surrounded now. When you leave here, you'll be taking her out of the state and not back to her apartment. No, her apartment is positively out of the question. She'll leave the state, kicking and screaming, if necessary, but she'll be gone today."

Devon was confused. What would cause the chief to react like this? He was talking in circles. "Chief, why does she need more protection? Once she gets to her uncle's house, even I would have a hard time getting in there. It's a fortress."

Chief Parker ignored his question. "Agent Walker, I need you to keep your cool with what you're about to see. I know your temper, and I won't put up with it right now."

Devon shifted from leg to leg. Yes, many had warned Parker about his temper, but there was something in his boss's expression that made his heart race. "Chief, what's going on?"

Chief Parker sighed, then reached over and turned the knob of the door to the office. "Follow me."

As soon as he switched on the light, nausea swelled up the back of Devon's throat. They were everywhere. On every wall and window, there were photos of Mary. Some were even of her and Devon together in the apartment. Yates had known where she was the whole time and had been following them. He had photos of him leaving her apartment and Matthews showing up. There were even photos looking into the apartment that were taken when the door opened. On the wall facing the door was a blown-up photo of Mary as a child. It was the one the newspapers ran right after Yates murdered her parents. He'd circled her face in red, and written below it, "found you, little mouse."

Chapter 15

Devon turned and ran out the door, ignoring the chief screaming his name. Matthews was already standing by Devon's car, waiting for him. Devon didn't have to say anything. Matthews got in the passenger seat and was ready to go. He broke every traffic regulation on the way to the congressman's house. Matthews tried multiple times to call Mary's phone, but no one was answering. None of the guards were answering their phones either, neither was anyone at the house. Something was wrong. Devon felt in the pit of his stomach that Mary was in danger, and he wasn't there to protect her. He'd kill Yates with his bare hands if he hurt one hair on her head.

His heart almost stopped when he turned the last corner, and the road was full of flashing lights and a coroner's van. Matthews leaned over the seat and tried to grab him before he jumped out of the car, but was too slow. Matthews climbed out and ran after Devon. He knew he needed to stop him in case it was Mary the coroner was here for.

"Walker, dude, you need to stay calm. Let's find out what happened before you go off the deep end," he yelled to his partner.

Devon wasn't listening as he ran around the side of the house where the officers clustered. There were two bodies on the sidewalk covered with sheets. He could see blood pooling around them. He went up to the first body and ripped the sheet off before anyone could stop him. One of the local officers started yelling at Devon, but stopped when he flashed his badge.

The first body he recognized as one of the guards. Matthews caught up to him before he could reach the second. "Walker, stop. The media vans are starting to show up. You need to calm down. Let me look at the second body while you go find the person who called this in. Get some answers and information before you lose all control." Devon didn't want to listen to his partner, but knew he was right.

Matthews came over to him as he found the responding officer. "The other body was the second photo you sent me earlier today. It's not Mary. I ran into Smitty with forensics and they're not hopeful about finding anything either. Assuming it was Yates, he didn't even follow his normal MO. He killed the guards and didn't take their faces. Being out in the open, whoever did this opted for a quick kill. It was most likely a snatch and grab, and the guards got in the way of them getting to Mary."

A sudden wail came from inside the house. Both men turned on their toes towards it. It was Mary's aunt. The officer that had just finished interviewing her came out to talk to Walker and Matthews. "She saw some of what happened. She said she's been watching out the window for her niece to arrive when all hell broke loose. Once the security car pulled up, she ran to the back door to let them in. Before she reached the door, she heard the guards shouting. She ran to the side window to see down the pathway and was only able to see a person covered from head-to-toe throw Mary over their shoulder and rush back to a red Ford Focus and drive off. She wasn't able to get a look at their face, so she wasn't able to identify if it was Yates." The officer finished and rushed off to where another officer was calling for him.

Matthews turned to Walker. "We need to consider that this may not have been Yates. The congressman has enemies, and lots of them. But it's good news that Mary was taken and not killed. That means the abductor, whoever it is, wants something and shouldn't harm Mary right away. That'll give us time to find her, Walker. We need to be smart about this. I need you in agent mode, not acting like a jealous lover. When you lose your cool, mistakes happen. Mistakes that won't help us find Mary. So, are you good?"

Was he good? Hell no, he wasn't good. He was going to do things to Yates that would make Satan blush when he got ahold of him, but he needed to be strong for Mary. He'd worry about revenge after they found her.

"Yeah, I'm good." Everything Matthews was saying made sense, but that didn't make Devon feel any better. That psycho had Mary. He knew with every fiber in his being it was Yates. He could be doing anything to her, and they have no clue where he'd gone. The FBI and MPD had been trying to locate him since he came back on the scene a month ago, after eluding them for years. But that was before. They didn't have Mary's work. Or Devon, who'd move heaven and hell to find her.

He knew Mary had turned her home office into a tell-all of Yate's life. He tried to give her the space she needed, thinking that having something to focus on would help channel the stress of knowing Yates was out there somewhere waiting to get his hands on her. But maybe he should have paid more attention. If he'd been more involved, Mary might have resented the intrusion, but he may have been able to prevent Yates from getting his hands on her in the first place. His agent training was telling him Yates would never back down in his pursuit, even if it took years. Mary would never be safe as long as Yates was free.

He was sure, with all the work she had done to dissect Yates's mind, there would be something there to give them at least a head start on where to look. Maybe he would see something Mary didn't. It was his job to put clues together. "Matthews let's go. We need to get back to Mary's apartment. She may have stumbled onto something that'll help us find Yates. We need to move fast. You call the chief on the way. He may want to send more people. Hell, he can send the whole bureau if it'll help."

Devon was already getting into the car when his phone rang. "Agent Walker, where the hell did you go? I called you and told you I needed you here. I went looking for you after you ran off and was told by a patrol officer that you got in your car and drove away even after I ordered you to stay put." The chief sounded irritated.

Did his chief really think he wouldn't race off to get Mary back into his custody? Noticing how Matthews was looking at him, he tried to curb his temper. "Mary's missing. Her security detail was attacked and murdered outside the congressman's house. Yates has her. We need to find her. I'm not going to waste my time at a crime scene that hasn't even been gone over by forensics yet. I'm going to work at another angle."

Devon could hear the chief cursing under his breath. Maybe Devon had finally gotten his attention. "The director is going to have my ass." He paused briefly, "What's your new angle?"

Devon clenched his jaw, and his knuckles turned white as he gripped the steering wheel. The chief's first words after being told about Mary were only to worry about himself, not for the fact Mary was in grave danger. He needed to keep his cool, though, or the chief would pull rank and pull him from the investigation. He wasn't that stupid. The chief had a way of being petty when he felt cornered, when Devon's temper flared. The chief would have just cause to pull Devon for being too close to the victim, but there was no way he'd allow him to pull him from the case. This was Mary, *his* Mary. "Listen Chief, Mary was working on understanding Yates's behavior patterns, and whatever else a forensic psychologist looks for. Matthews and I are heading back to her apartment now to look over her work. If you know anyone that may understand this information better than me, send them over. She's been working on this almost non-stop for a month. I bet she has information we can use."

The line was silent for a moment. "If she's been working on it for over a month, why am I just now hearing about it? Maybe we could've helped sooner, and this wouldn't have happened. What were you thinking, Agent Walker, keeping this from the FBI? If this doesn't end well, I'll have your badge."

Now Devon was pissed. He had the audacity to insinuate Devon was the blame for Mary's kidnapping. Hell no. He'd try to ignore the chief's idle threats, for Mary's sake. "She didn't even want me to know what she was working on. Every time I tried to get into her office, or ask her what she thought about it, she always said it was something for her classes. The only reason I know what she was doing was that one night I was curious. So after she went to sleep, I picked the lock of her office and found information about Yates all over the place. If she knew I broke into her office, I would've lost her trust, and that was something I wasn't willing to do. Losing her trust would've only made her more distant and harder to protect. "

"Yeah, okay, got it. I'll send a few agents over that might be able to help. This needs to be an all hands on deck situation. Now, I gotta go talk to the congressman. He's called me four times, now I know why. I can't put him off any longer. Just get me something I can work with."

The chief hung up before Devon could respond, but the chief was right. It had to be all hands on deck. If Yates harmed Mary, he would skin him alive.

Once they were back in the apartment, Matthews let out a low whistle as they stepped into Mary's office. There was a lot more information posted than the last time Devon was inside the room. Sometime, in the last two weeks, Mary covered almost every inch of free space with some sort of information about Yates or his tendencies. They all knew Yates was considered a family annihilator, and Mary was determined to dissect his every known move. It was the children that gave Mary nightmares. She couldn't understand why Yates would murder the children. This information must have been tearing her apart. She was always trying to keep her emotions bottled up inside. Maybe that's why she'd been a little distant lately. Devon knew what kind of sick people were out in the world, but even after what happened to Mary as a child, she still couldn't fathom pure, unadulterated evil in people. At the mere mention of Yates, she started crying and whispering about the children. Yates needed to be stopped. Only then could Mary's nightmare be over.

Devon and Matthews dug into the information Mary provided when one thing stood out, highlighted on multiple pages. A family annihilator was never spontaneous. Which made sense with everything they already knew about Yates. He stalked his victims long enough to know when the entire family would be home. And he'd never missed anyone until Mary. Family annihilators were most often family members, and it usually ended in murder-suicides, but not in Yates's case. Mary had information circled on multiple papers that a family annihilator usually had issues in one or more of four distinct categories. They had their work cut out for them. They had to figure out what categories Yates fell into.

"Hey Matthews, come see this," Devon yelled. Pointing to the papers on the wall and moving over so they'd both be able to look. "A family annihilator can be considered a self-righteous killer. These killers target mothers as the responsibility for the breakdown of a family. Most of their anger will be directed at the mother, but also towards the children of the women. This doesn't mention fathers or male figures." Devon put a sticky note with an 'X' on that one. "A family annihilator can be considered a disappointed killer. These killers believe they are the ones that were let down by the family, and, therefore, the entire family needs to pay."

"That couldn't be Yates. He wasn't related to any of his victims." Matthews pointed out as Devon placed another 'X' note.

"A family annihilator can be considered an anomic killer. These killers latch onto a family they believe causes the killer to have economic success, but then took that success away, such as in bankruptcy. The killer will then believe the family has no purpose and will target them.

"Last, a family annihilator can be considered a paranoid killer. These killers believe they are protecting their own families or others from those they perceive as a threat." Tapping the last paper, he pointed back to the description. "This is the one I think Yates would be classified as. It's the only one that makes sense. He somehow feels threatened by his victims, so in his mind, that would give him cause to murder the entire family."

Looking around the room, they could see Mary was trying to determine which category Yates's victims fell into. If they could confirm their suspicion, they could determine how Yates picked his victims. If Yates followed his past patterns, he already had another family on his radar. The only unknown factor would be if he halted his hunting to kidnap Mary. If that was the case, they were at another dead end.

By the time the other agents arrived, Mary's office looked like a labyrinth of red string. Devon and Matthews had connected one side of the room to the other for fear of moving anything she had posted up. While they didn't know why she hung those papers where she did, someone else might, and disturbing her arrangement could compromise the meaning.

The new agents on the scene watched as the two men stretched bullet projection strings from one point of the room to another. Taping the ends to the wall, the strings twined into veins where information overlapped. They were desperate to find anything that pointed them in the right direction. Devon motioned for the other agents to come in and help. They needed more eyes.

Chapter 16

Mary's head hurt like the devil. What the hell happened? Where was she? The events were slowly coming back to her. They were on her uncle's property, so no one else should have been able to get past their security. For that reason, the security detail must not have been as vigilant. They'd just exited the vehicle and were moving up the sidewalk to her uncle's home when she heard a grunt and saw one of the security guards fall to the ground. The other security guard yelled for her to run and get to the house, but she mustn't have moved fast enough. She remembers turning to run when she felt a sharp pain at the base of her skull. Then everything went dark. Looking around the dimly lit, musty smelling room, Mary didn't see either of the security guards, and knew she was completely alone.

As soon as she regained her bearings, she understood exactly what had happened. It had to be Yates. He had finally got her and made good on his promise to finish what he had failed at many years ago. Yates said he didn't forget her, and so he proved he had found her. Would he kill her quickly? Would he kill her like he killed her parents? She trembled. Was it from fear or anger?

Knowing what a monster he was, and knowing what he did to his victims, she prayed it didn't make her a coward to hope for a quick death. Would he end up taking her face as well? Her poor aunt and uncle, they must be frantic. Thank goodness she didn't remember seeing her parents after he got done butchering them, but she did see photos from other crime scenes. The investigator her uncle recommended when she explained she was on a crusade to gather more information was reluctant to send over photos from some of Yates's earlier murders. How he got them, she had no idea. She didn't think the investigator even realized how it would affect her, having lived through it herself.

Mary had to push all those feelings out of her head and focus on getting out of wherever he'd taken her. She needed to focus on her survival. Looking around, she tried to find any clue to help her figure out where she was being held. Due to her unwillingness to play into any of his games, which will infuriate him more, Yates might finally get what he wanted and kill her. Which might be better than whatever he has planned for her.

Her wrists and ankles, bound by rope, were unable to move from the metal loop anchor point cemented into the floor. She pulled, but the loop was secure. There was no way for her to break her binds. If only she could find something small and thin, she could use it as a friction point to saw at the rope and break the threads. She taught herself all sorts of helpful skills over the years. She was determined never to be a victim again, but that didn't seem to help this time. The room was dirty, but not cluttered. Which meant there would be nothing for her to use to get free or as a weapon. But she was older than the last time she encountered Yates, and she was more prepared. She'd go down swinging if it came to that.

She waited for what seemed like days before the coward showed himself. "So, you finally decided to wake up? I barely hit you, but you've been out for hours. So inconvenient. You're such a weakling. I will break you, you know. I've had many years to dream about how I'll make you pay for not coming out of your hiding place to play with me the first time we met. If you had obeyed me then, I would've made it easy on you, but not now. You've made me wait a very long time for this, and because you made me wait, I think we'll spend some nice quality time together. How does that sound? Would you like me to tell you in very graphic detail everything I've dreamed of doing to you? Wait, I think telling you will make the fun less rewarding. I think I'll just show you how much frustration you've caused me over the years. Maybe if you beg me to kill you, I'll oblige. Although, your mother begged, and I still gutted her. We'll just have to wait and see, won't we?" His dark silhouette straightened away from the door and moved to sit directly in front of her. He was muttering to himself, but Mary couldn't make out the words.

She didn't want to show weakness. To show weakness would be to give the bastard what he wanted. Mary was stronger than him, and she would prove it. But how long would she need to hold out? She knew the police and FBI were searching for her at that very moment, but they'd been tracking Yates for years, to no avail. Maybe if she would've shared her information with someone, even Devon, they may have been able to catch him before this. But no, she had to work it out on her own. Stubborn. Always so freaking stubborn. Now look where she was.

Time stood still as Yates played his game with her. He was true to his word. And it was evident the years had brought him immense frustration. He began his games slowly, starting off by throwing small pebbles about the size of marbles. As he threw the pebbles, they hit her legs, then her torso, and finally her face and head. She soon felt like one big bruise, and there were multiple cuts and scrapes covering any exposed skin.

As time went on, the stones got larger. Instead of marble sized, they were the size of golf balls and did much more damage. With an entire bucket of rocks by his side, he wasn't running out of ammunition any time soon. And every few minutes, he would get up with his bucket, and go around the room, picking up the stones and whistling. "Mary, do you know where the punishment of stoning originated from?" He asked, with a smile on his face and excitement in his voice.

Mary averted her eyes to the ground. She didn't want to talk to his bastard or even look at him. Besides, she was already using all her energy not to break down and ask him to kill her. She wasn't that weak, though. It's just that it was becoming so hard to stay strong.

"Okay, since you don't know, I'll tell you. In the Bible, they used capital punishment for a variety of offenses. Some offenses were murder, adultery, rape, disobedience to one's parents, witchcraft, and idolatry. It's only fitting that I carry out this punishment for you. I think you'd qualify for the offense of witchcraft. That's the only explanation I have as to why your parents wouldn't tell me where you were hiding all those years ago. It takes a very strong person to withstand the pain that I put your parents through, but they still wouldn't talk. Believe me, I pulled out every little trick in my repertoire to make them talk. It had to be witchcraft. Why else would they have given up their lives for a scraggly little brat? In the end, they would've died anyway, but they didn't know that. Tell me something. What spell did you put on them?" He continued talking as he still threw rocks. Finally, a rock hit her temple with enough force that sweet darkness consumed her, temporarily ending her suffering.

She mustn't have been out long, because when she woke up, Yates was still sitting on the floor in front of her, tossing and catching a rock up and down. "We're going to need to try something else. It won't be any fun if you aren't nice and awake while we play our games. For a moment there, I thought I may have killed you. I was a little upset with myself, because I have so much more in store for you. If I would've killed you, I wouldn't be able to continue my games, and that's unacceptable. Boy, do I have so many more games for us to play together. I think the next game I have in mind will keep you very alert."

He stood up and walked behind her. He was only out of sight for a moment when she suddenly felt overcome with freezing cold water. It took all her willpower not to scream. He slowly walked back in front of her, smiling. Moving behind a pillar, he brought out a large metal fan. After he turned it on, she felt like she'd stepped outside into a winter storm, without a jacket and right out of the shower. It was horrible.

"Let's see if that'll keep you awake for a while."

Walking to the other side of the room, he sat down with a newspaper, and hummed *It's A Small World*. Just when her shivering seemed to slow, he got up and threw another bucket of water on her. Mary finally spotted a little spigot in the wall and knew he wouldn't run out of water any time soon. She couldn't stop shivering, her heart was racing to keep blood moving to her extremities. It hurt to breathe, and she lost feeling in her hands and feet. Confusion was setting in. If he kept at this pace, hallucinations would start, and her breathing would become so labored it would damage her organs. If she reached that level, it would be hard to recover. For a moment, she wished she didn't have the extensive knowledge of cold weather injuries. It made each symptom seem worse knowing what was coming next.

It seemed like hours before he finally shut off the fan. "I'm getting bored. I need another hands-on game to play." He looked like he was thinking about it for a moment, but she knew he already had decided what he was going to do with her. From what she gathered about him, he probably had everything planned out to the last detail. He wouldn't want to waste precious time on planning when he could be torturing her instead. She just hoped she could last until help came for her. Or until death took her. Death didn't seem like a bad option at the moment. She'd be able to see her parents again. She didn't have time to contemplate the benefits of death before the torment resumed.

His next method was definitely hands-on. He moved away from the water and walked behind her. She didn't know what was coming next and didn't have time to brace herself as he rustled with something and then a plastic bag dropped over her head as he tried to suffocate her. With her hands bound, there was nothing she could do to protect herself. This was worse than the stoning. As soon as she saw black spots and started to sway, he removed the bag from her head. It only stopped long enough for her to catch her breath, then it was back over her head again. She wasn't sure how long this went on, but it seemed like it would never end.

Her head snapped back as his fist connected with her left cheek. "Mary, Mary, Mary. You're disappointing me again. With every new game, you're getting weaker. Do you want me to tell you some fun facts about the games we're playing now?"

She couldn't control her anger. "No, you sick bastard! I don't want to hear all about your little games, you sadist. Why don't you make it fair and untie me? We can go one on one and see who the stronger one really is. Unless you're scared that I'll beat you. Come on," she screamed.

"Now, now. That outburst was uncalled for. We're just having a little bit of fun." He reached over and patted her hair. It took everything in her not to vomit at his touch, and he didn't like it when she physically recoiled. He let her know his displeasure with another punch to the face. This time, she saw stars. "Ungrateful bitch. Fine, we'll continue to play. I don't care if you seem uninterested in knowing more fun facts. I'm going to tell you, anyway. This game is called dry boarding. I already had fun with water, so waterboarding was off the table, so I decided to try this instead. Also, I like the idea of being able to see your expressions and feel your life leaving your body, and I wouldn't be able to do that with a towel over your face. I never thought death by asphyxiation was a rewarding one, but I think I'm changing my mind. Shall we continue?"

Before she had time to mutter a word, the bag was back over her head. This time, he kept it on a little longer than he should've, and once again, sweet darkness consumed her.

Slowly coming to, she knew he was sitting in front of her again. She sensed him and heard him fumbling with that damn plastic bag. "How remiss of me. I think I got a little carried away. It's that mouth of yours. You should really be nicer to me. At first, I couldn't feel a pulse on that scrawny neck of yours and thought for sure I killed you. I was just about to perform CPR, since I'm not done playing yet, but I was finally able to feel a pulse. As much as I'm sure you'd love my hands on you. It makes me physically ill thinking about my mouth on yours. No, I think

I would've just let you die if your will to live hadn't brought you back to me. But it did bring you back, and now we can have some more fun.

"I think the next game we'll play will be a little safer. Safer for me, that is, not for you. With this next game, there won't be a chance for me to 'accidentally' kill you. But you will wish you were dead. Hopefully, with this next game, I'll be able to make you lose your mind. We're going to play a game that is very popular with your U.S. Military at Guantanamo and your CIA. But don't worry, we are just going to listen to a little music. How does that sound?" He reached into his pockets and pulled out ear plugs. He was inserting them into his ears as he moved to a radio against the wall.

She heard a small click a fraction of a second before she heard the most torturing sound she could ever imagine. When Yates said he was going to play a game in common with the CIA and that it would be music, she was expecting some of the songs mentioned in interviews as being used, none of which could compare to this hell. The sounds playing over the stereo were that of tortured screams. Just scream after scream after scream. Yates could write the handbook on torture.

This was the one that would be her undoing. She wasn't able to hold it together for even a few minutes. No matter how much she tried, because she was bound, she wasn't about to cover her ears with her hands, or even lift her shoulders to muffle that sound. So the screams kept coming. Within minutes, she was curled into her knees and sobbing like a little girl. Before putting her head down, she noticed Yates was smiling. He was thoroughly enjoying watching her break, and this would be the one to make her shatter completely apart. The screaming kept going; and it didn't matter how she tried to cover her ears, she could still hear the terror in those screams. At some point, Yates left the room, but she didn't know how long he'd be gone. She would rather have the stoning, freezing, or even the dry boarding over this torture.

Her body was breaking down when the so-called song finally stopped. Even though the screaming had ended on the radio, she could still hear it in her head. No matter how much time she had left before he killed her, she knew she would still hear those screams. If by chance a miracle happened and Devon, someone, anyone, found her, she'd hear those screams every day for the rest of her life.

Yates stared down at her, withering like a cockroach. Letting out a laugh that was full of pure joy. This wasn't normally how he tortured his victims, but it was much more fun. In the future, he may need to rethink his strategies. And he needed more time with his victim, which required a bit of arrangement, but it wasn't impossible. What he needed to do was move quickly before she regained strength between games. Looking down at Mary, all pathetic, he gave her a swift kick to get her attention. The kick didn't seem to faze her, or get her attention, so he gave her a few more, focusing on the ribs. Slowly, the sobbing subsided, and she moved to look at him.

Glassy, unseeing eyes stared up, and he knew he was on the verge of winning. But he was far from done with her. The fact this bitch eluded him for over twenty years had tortured him every day. He deserved to make her pay for ruining his life. No, he wasn't done with her yet, not by a long shot. He gave her one more kick for good measure.

"Are you ready for your next game, Mary?" Giving her a false sense of hope, he stated, "Maybe after this next one, I'll let you rest a bit. No

use torturing you if you're dead. Do you want to have more fun? I do."
He didn't expect an answer, but he continued to talk, anyway. "Now,
what other fun games can we play? We could break a few bones. I could
force feed you until you pop. Impalement always intrigued me. I could
be like Vlad. I could be like a mobster and do a tooth extraction." Shaking his head, "No, I don't think getting too close to your mouth is such
a good idea. You'd probably try to take a bite out of me, just like the
little rodent you are." He threw his finger in the air and exclaimed, "I
got it! Let's see if witches bleed red."

Chapter 17

It took all his self-control not to rip down every red string or tear every piece of paper to shreds. They were getting nowhere, and Devon knew time was running out. There was always a method to a person's madness. He just couldn't figure out Mary's. The information jumped around and there was no method to it at all. She must have had help to gather this information, and he needed to find out who helped her. He had a hunch it was the congressman, but would the congressman tell Devon what he wanted to know? Of course he would. His niece was missing, and he had made clear to Chief Parker that he'd provide any help he could offer. Pulling out his phone, he quickly dialed his boss's number.

Not fifteen minutes later, he had the name of the private investigator the congressman used to help Mary gather information. Mr. Franklin Simon, private detective. The first time he called the number, no one answered, and he left a not so polite message. When he called back five minutes later, Mr. Simon answered. "Agent Walker, I just got off the phone with Congressman Carter and he said I'm to share any information I have with you."

"Yeah, well, that would be helpful. Thank you so much for your co-operation. It's not like a woman's life is at stake or anything." Devon's words radiated sarcasm. Of course, he'd need to check with his employer. It's not like this is a matter of life or death. This was an FBI case and people should tell him what he needs to know. He knew that's not how things worked, but he wasn't thinking rationally. Nothing about his way of thinking was rational when it came to Mary.

"Agent Walker, please do not be crass. Just a moment ago, I received notification of the situation and I'm ready to help. I have a few boxes of information that I think you might find helpful. I've kept copies of all the information I provided to Ms. Anderson, per instructions from the congressman. Would you like to come to my office, or do you want me to meet you somewhere else?"

"Bring the information to Ms. Anderson's apartment. I want to compare it to what she has here. Do you need the address?"

"No, I have the address. Mr. Carter gave me that information when he told me to put myself completely at your disposal. The congressman wants apprised of any information we can link to his niece's disappearance, and I want you to know that I agreed and won't hold anything back from him. Give me twenty minutes and I should be at your location."

As Devon hung up the phone, for the first time since Mary disappeared, he felt hopeful. With any luck, Mr. Simon had something in those boxes that would help them locate Mary. But if he had information that could help, why didn't Mary put it together? Maybe because she wasn't an investigator. She's a professor. Well, between him and Matthews, they'd find the link if it was in that mound of information. If it wasn't there, he'd find it himself. They needed to find Mary, and fast.

Every second she was missing was eating away at him. He was supposed to protect her. If he hadn't left her, she'd still be safe, tucked away in her apartment. The chief called him to do his job, and he couldn't fault him for it. He was still an FBI agent, but he wasn't being reasonable at all when it came to Mary. He should've argued with Parker, and the job be damned. It was meaningless compared to Mary's life. Her safety should've come first. He let her down, but hopefully he'd have a chance to ask for forgiveness.

Chapter 18

Mary was losing consciousness again. Yates made sure every time she was awake, he gave her another cut or two. Whatever her body could handle before she passed out again. He promised she would die by lingchi, or better known as 'the death by a thousand cuts'. This was by far the most painful torture he had performe. And from what he was saying, it would be the last one. The one that would kill her. He even described how he'd be able to slice her face off without killing her. Slice by slice over a long period of time.

Of course, he wouldn't give her the gift of a quick kill. He meant for her to suffer. Apparently, this torture practice came from the early 10th century in China and continued until banned in 1905. He liked to give her little history lessons on top of the physical torture. Hearing his voice was torture enough.

Mary knew she had a good chance of survival if the FBI was able to find her soon. But she didn't know how much more her body could physically or mentally take. While the body could lose fifteen percent of the total blood volume rapidly and still survive, Yates was cutting her little by little, so it may have been slow enough for her body to repro-duce some of the lost blood, since the blood was always regenerating.

He also wasn't going deep, just short, little slices like paper cuts on steroids.

He told her he was determined to make one thousand cuts before peeling off her face and then the finale of slitting her throat. He promised to put her face alongside the faces of her parents. As he announced that, her stomach muscles cramped, and if she'd been able to, she would have doubled over in pain. Turning her face as far away as she could, the bile rose, and she couldn't hold it down. The faces of his victims had never been located. This monster had dozens of faces from innocent victims stashed somewhere, including her parents, and now he was gloating about it. There was a special place in hell reserved for people like him.

She lost count at one hundred cuts. And counting them made the pain worse. She knew she had a while until he reached one thousand, but how could she last that long? The cut he made on the top of her thigh hurt so badly it made her pass out.

When she woke up, she wondered if it wouldn't be better if he'd just end it now. She'd asked herself that very question so many times over the last hours. Or days? Mary wasn't exactly sure how long she'd been there. Time stood still. She needed to be stronger than Yates and hold out until help could arrive. She had to be optimistic that help would eventually come and not lose her faith. Hopefully, they won't be too late. Even if they were, if they caught Yates, in her mind, her sacrifice would be worth it. Mentally, she was strong, but how could she be physically strong when she was in so much pain? Mind over matter. She needed to push the pain aside. That was easier said than done.

Going crazy was more likely to happen before her body physically broke down. Yates had to be a master at torture to continue the way he did. He hummed *'It's A Small World'* over and over while he was cutting her. If she made it out of there, she never wanted to hear that blasted song ever again. He looked her in the eyes and smiled during the process. If she looked away, he would stab her rather than making a little slice. This was the man who killed her parents, and so many other families. She wouldn't let him kill her, too. She would be his failure again, and she was determined to be the reason he got caught.

But what pulled her through the agony more than anything was thinking about Devon. She knew he was out there tearing the city apart to find her, and he wouldn't stop until he did. She worried about her poor aunt and uncle and the pain this must be causing them. Right now, though, she needed to find a happy place in her mind. Maybe then she'd be able to endure the pain. She tried to think of her dream island, the one she told Devon about, her place of pure safety. It would have high cliffs, and only one inlet for boats to enter. For people passing by the island, it would look impenetrable. For her, the island meant safety. Her aunt and uncle would live there, along with anyone else they wanted. Maybe even Devon.

They would live in a little island bungalow with great views of the sand and crystal blue waters. The waters had to be crystal clear, or Mary wouldn't be able to step foot into them. The island would also have a waterfall, and so many birds and they could sit on the porch and listen to the music they sang. Yes, this is what she'd try to think about instead of what was being done to her. Her happy place—with Devon.

Devon was so desperate, he was about to go door to door and tear every house apart until he found Mary. He was ready to call the chief when Matthews yelled to him from Mary's office. "Walker, we found something!" Devon ran into the office and Matthews was shaking papers, and Mr. Simon had a big smile on his face. "We did it, Walker! We found the link. Now let's go get this bastard."

Chapter 19

As the darkness faded, Yates came into view through her bleary vision. He sat on the floor in front of her, staring at her again. "Oh, so nice of you to join me. I want to tell you a story, Mary. Do you want to hear it?"

"No, you bastard. I don't want to hear anything you have to tell me."

He cocked his head to the side and stared at her like he was studying her. "No? Not even the story of why I killed your parents?"

It was killing her not to lash out, but Mary remained silent. Yes, she wanted to know why he killed her parents, but she knew he was relishing in her pain. Granted, right now, she didn't much care if he was going to gain pleasure in her pain or not. She was on the verge of finding out why her parents were his target. This was the 'why' question that plagued her for as long as she could remember. Why her family? From all the stories she's heard, her parents never hurt anyone in all their lives. They didn't deserve to have theirs cut short by some psychopath with a knife and fascination with death.

"Okay. I'll take your silence as confirmation you want to hear my story." He moved around as if trying to get comfortable. He reached behind him and produced a stone.

She involuntarily flinched. Yates saw the motion and the corner of his mouth turned up into a lopsided grin.

Was he going to throw them at her again? She kept an eye on his hands, and it looked like he was just rolling it around and didn't plan on throwing it at her. Yet.

He noticed the terrified look on her face as she focused on the stone. Yates relished in knowing a simple motion could strike fear into this heartless bitch. "So, now onto my story. It all started when I was a little boy. My father went out for milk one night, and never came back. It was about a year later that my mother told me he was killed in a dark alley trying to score some drugs. Most mothers would try to shield their children from such horrors, but not my dear old mom. She wanted me to know what trash my father was. When she wanted to hurt me, she'd tell me I'm just like him and I'll also never amount to anything. She remarried suddenly, and this guy was worse than my dad, by far. He didn't last though, and neither did the next one.

"They'd tire of my mother after only a few months, then leave us high and dry. With each marriage, the men got meaner and more abusive. The only time I'd be able to avoid the beatings by the current stepfather was when I was at school or the library. The library became a safe haven for me after school. Isn't that sad? Instead of having a normal childhood running around with friends and playing sports, I spent mine just trying to stay out of striking range of mom's latest husband. My mother married her fourth husband when I was only seven years old. By the time I was eight, I realized what a bastard he was. When my mother

153

wasn't around for him to beat on, I was his target. So, I tried to distance myself from him as much as possible and wouldn't leave the library until closing time every night.

"When I was twelve years old, I decided I was done taking the abuse. After being his punching bag for five miserable years, I was finally done. He didn't leave after a short time like all the others, so I made a decision. He had to go. Now I just needed to figure out how I was going to do it. Back in those days, we didn't have the internet. So, guess what I did? I went to the library and researched the great serial killers of times past. Some books I found were great. Some were almost like 'how to' books about being a successful serial killer. I learned so much just sitting on the floor in the back of the library reading about Clementine Barnabet, Boone Helm, Edmund Kemper, The Bender family, and Ed Gein, just to name a few. I found out how they killed, why they killed, and what happened that led them to being caught.

"I found that killing was actually very easy. It was making sure you didn't make mistakes that would lead the police to you that was the hard part. But I was a very smart kid. I knew my plan would be so fool-proof that those cops would never catch me. You need to be a little more careful today than you did back then, because of the advances in forensic science. I miss the early days. Then again, I've been killing for over thirty years now, and even though the FBI knows who I am, they still can't catch me. Such incompetence.

"My step-father was my first kill. I was a little sloppy, but I had a great thought-out plan. It was a work of art. I planned everything down to the smallest detail. Since I've been spending so much time at the library, I used that as my alibi. After months of spending all my time after school at the library, the librarians, custodians, and even the regular customers knew my name, and said hello in passing. I found out where the library had dead spots on the cameras, and I spent my time there. I found one blind spot that was very close to an exit and spent a few weeks there, so people would get used to seeing me in that section and become complacent.

"On the day I killed my stepfather, I went to the library like normal, took a stack of books from a shelf, and spread them across a table. It was common for me to roam the library even after I had books selected. I made my area look like I was still there, just somewhere around the building, and I snuck out the side exit. Our house was only a ten-minute walk from the library, but that day I made it in five by running. My step-dad was more or less always drunk by five p.m., and I was just in luck. Today was also one of those days. My mom was at work, so it was only him at home. I snuck up behind his recliner chair in the living room and cut his throat. It was messy, because I wasn't sure how deep to cut, and I went a little overboard. It ended up looking like I was trying to cut his head clean off his body.

"The bastard didn't even move. I learned from that, too. Next time, I wanted the person to know it was me that was ending their miserable life. What satisfaction was there in the person not knowing who ended their wretched lives? They would know I was the one who outsmarted them before they died.

"Since I was completely covered in blood, I quickly showered and rushed back to the library before anyone noticed I was gone. I placed my bloody clothes in a trash bag and dropped them in a trash can outside the library. No one would think to look there for evidence since it was so far away from the crime scene. Sneaking back into the library was easy. I just made my way to where the bathrooms were and made sure they saw me saying hello to the employees.

"By the time I sat back down, I had only about forty-five minutes until closing time. Once 7pm came around, I gathered my backpack, put my books away, and said good night to the maintenance man locking up. Taking my time on the way home, I thought about what I would say when I had to call 9-1-1. Sounding happy would be an indicator of guilt, but would I be able to keep the excitement out of my voice? After rehearsing so many scenarios on the way home, I was ready. Just like a play, I practiced many dialogues.

"All that thinking and practicing ended up being for nothing. The police were already at my house when I got home. Now it was time for me to act. I ran up to the taped off area and tried to push through. When the officer grabbed my arm and told me I had to stay back, I cried that it was my house, and I wanted my mommy. The officer called over his radio, then led me to his cruiser. He said my mom was on her way over and to wait for her there. He let me sit in the front and he walked back to the line to keep people from crossing.

"Mom finally found me, and she was sobbing. It took everything I had not to laugh right in her face.'Jimmy. Oh, Jimmy. It's so horrible. He's gone. Someone killed him. What are we going to do?' She whined to me. She acted like I was supposed to care that the abusive bastard was dead. I didn't say anything, I just reached up and gave mom a hug. I put my face into the side of her neck so she wouldn't see me smile. Evidently, the police didn't suspect me either because I wasn't apprehended as soon as I came home. They wouldn't be able to use prints, because I lived there, and my prints were everywhere. It was about a week later that an officer came by to apologize to my mother and explain that they still didn't have a person of interest.

"My stepfather was shady, and everyone that the police interviewed had an alibi. The police probably realized how much of a loser he was and didn't even try too hard to find his killer. He was a druggie and a drunk. So that's one less dirtbag on the streets. Good riddance is probably what they thought.

"The police said they were going to hold onto the case file, but it would be put aside for now pending new evidence. That worked well for me, since I was the one who slit his throat, and maybe soon I'll get to show you just how I did it. How would you like that, Mary?"

"You're sick," she whispered. "Why the families? Why the children? No matter what you think the parents did, the children were innocent. Why couldn't you just leave them alone? You're vile, pure evil."

He ignored her outburst. "Oh, yes. I almost forgot. That was actually where I was going with this. How do I pick my victims? It's very simple, really. I go back to the library I spent so much time at as a child and wait for people to look at the same books that were like a haven for me. If someone is interested in serial killers, I introduce them to a real live one. *Me*.

"I know what you're thinking, but only sick people are interested in killers. Right? So, I do the only thing that makes sense. I get rid of the sickness before it can spread within the rest of the family. Though I guess I could just focus on the individual that's already exhibiting the sickness. I just can't take any chances of having it spread to all members in a household. And that, my dear, is why I also kill the children. If the sickness is in one parent, they may have passed it down to a child. If I didn't take care of them right away, I may need to come back years later

157

and finish the job. So, you see, I'm being efficient. I really don't need any competition, now do I? I'm doing society a favor really by not allowing more people like myself to run around."

She had a hard time comprehending what he was saying. So, it was all about what someone read that determined if he killed them? How was that logical? She studied serial killers, and there was nothing wrong with her. "What about my parents, then? They didn't read that stuff. They weren't 'sick', as you call it."

He giggled. "Oh, but they did; and they were. Your mother was the one that was reading a book on the Co-ed killer, Edmund Kemper. He's one of my favorites, even though he ended up being stupid. At first, I was confused when your mother picked up the book. It was usually the men that read those books, so it intrigued me. I knew the moment I saw your mother that she was going to be special. As soon as she left, I went and found the book she was reading.

"Edmund Kemper was amazing. Media dubbed him the Co-ed Killer. He killed his grandparents when he was only fifteen years old. He told the police he wanted to know how it felt to kill his grandmother. And then he killed his grandfather because he knew he'd be mad that he killed his grandmother. He later killed, dismembered, and assaulted six female hitchhikers, then lastly killed his mother and her friend. Unfortunately, Kemper was very weak. He turned himself into the police. If he was smart, he could've kept on killing for years without being apprehended. I'm smart, so the police will never catch me. So don't get your hopes up for a rescue. And I sure as shit won't be weak enough to turn myself in. If they want me, they need to work for it.

"They've been searching for years and have never even gotten close to me. Well, actually, they have come in close proximity to me, but I was invisible. I've actually been living in the house next door to your childhood home. Mr. Smith, your neighbor that so rudely interrupted me, had an untimely accident that allowed his home to come onto the market. I swooped in and got it for a steal. So you see, I'm invincible.

"That sucks for you because they'll never find you. You are going to be my guest for as long as I'm enjoying your company, unless I accidentally kill you. Which I've almost done a few times now. I might need to rethink some of our games. Of course, after I'm done with my fun, I can't just let you go. So, I think I'll be nice and reunite you with your family. Isn't that nice of me?"

She wouldn't allow herself to cry. She wouldn't show him weakness. "You're a bastard. That's what I know. Now tell me why you killed my parents. I can't believe it was because of a stupid book my mother read. That's ridiculous."

He let out a stomach churning laugh. Every time she heard the cackling of his joy, it made her nauseous. "Where was I? Oh yes, of course. I guess we got a bit off topic. We were talking about why I chose your family. Right? Well, I saw that your mother was looking at books on Edmund Kemper and got intrigued. Why I watched your family for longer than I do most others, I can't explain. But having watched them for about three weeks, I decided they needed to be cleansed.

After watching your home day and night, jotting down all yours and your parent's movements, I was ready to get to know you better. You were easy, you went to school, soccer practice, then home. Overall, you were a quiet little girl, with only a few friends. In those three weeks, I only saw one other little girl come over to your house. You were pathetic even back then. By the end of those three weeks, I knew what time your parents went to work, when they came home, weekly shopping trips, and what neighbors to watch for. I knew Mr. Smith could be a problem, but what were the chances he'd be an issue the day I chose to cleanse your house of sickness?

"The only thing I didn't count on, or plan for, was your parents hiding you away from me. That was really very naughty of them, and I made sure they knew my displeasure before I finished with them. Before I ended their miserable lives, I made sure they knew that if it was the last thing I did, I would gut their little girl. I told them the longer they kept you from me, the worse it would be when I found you. They both begged and begged for you to be spared. I was determined to make sure I would wipe every trace of them from this earth. Do you want me to tell you how your mother screamed and your father begged for me to spare your life?"

He took her silence as confirmation she indeed wanted to hear more. In truth, she couldn't have answered him if she wanted to. She felt like her heart was being ripped from her chest. She knew if she opened her mouth to speak, she would throw up, which would please Yates's ego.

"After I tied up your parents so they couldn't flee, I went in search of you. Little did I know, just like the little mouse you are, you were hiding in the walls. Your parents were stronger than I anticipated, and that infuriated me. With every little cut to your mother, I could see the fight leave dear old dad. Nevertheless, neither one would tell me what I wanted to know; the one thing that would end all their suffering. After telling them many times, if they would just tell me where you were, I would end their pain very quickly. They didn't know I lied to them and told them I would make your end quick and that you wouldn't suffer at all. Come to think about it, I don't think they believed me, probably because I told them I'd gut you when I found you. No one would expect you to be able to stay in your little hideaway with dear old mom and dad screaming and begging for your life. They were loud enough that I knew you'd be able to hear them from wherever you were hiding in the house.

"Your mother sobbed that she'd do anything I asked if I let you live, even become my whore. I made her think I was considering it up until the moment I stabbed her in the stomach and cut her throat. Then I finally ended your father's miserable life, but not before I made him watch as I removed your mother's face right in front of him. I explained to him that what I was doing to his wife was exactly what I was going to do to his daughter as soon as I caught her. That seemed to send a burst of adrenaline through him, but he still couldn't break his binds. And after hearing all that screaming, you still didn't come out of your hiding spot. Come to think of it, you may be more callous than I thought. You sacrificed your parents' lives just to save yourself. However, with every kill I've made since your parents, I remember their defiance. It has actually taken some of the joy out of cleansing households."

Callous? Sacrifice? Those screams haunted her nightmares and would haunt her until the day she died. Her parents prepared for every situation, even ones where survival was on the line. About a year before their deaths, they had told her if someone were to break into the house, and if she could, she needed to find a way to hide and not come out under any circumstance. No matter what she heard, she needed to stay hidden. Her parents would come get her when it was all clear. That's what she did that night. She hid and didn't come out. It's what her parents wanted.

But the things Yates was saying were making her doubt herself and her feelings about that night. That was it. Mary couldn't keep silent any longer. She couldn't listen to the filth coming out of his mouth. She

161

didn't want him to mention her parents again. Hearing their names come out of his mouth was like poison to her heart.

"Good. I'm glad you can no longer gain satisfaction over such a heinous act." Mary lashed out the only way she could, verbally. "My parents were good people that didn't deserve to die. I bet they are smiling down right now, knowing they caused your suffering. You're a bastard, and you won't win. Even if you kill me, you'll be doing me a favor by reuniting me with my parents, and you'll get caught. The people out looking for you are smarter and stronger than you, and you'll die. The only regret I have is that you'll probably die faster than you deserve. I didn't use to be a violent person, but I hope you suffer immensely before they put you down like a rabid animal.

"I'm not afraid to die. Are you? I know what awaits me when I leave this earth, and it gives me joy to imagine where you'll go. Lucifer will have you roasting on a spit just like a pig at a hog roast. All his demons will take turns peeling the flesh from your bones, and when they've taken every pound of flesh from your body, everything will magically be restored. Once you think the flaying and burning will end, it'll start all over again. A fitting eternal damnation for a pig like you."

She didn't even have time to brace herself before he reached out and struck her across the face. Her head slammed back with so much force she saw black spots and her breath escaped. "Bitch. You'll see how strong I am. I know all about your bleeding heart. How would you like it if I take you on my next cleanse? No, I know what I'll do. I'll go pick out another family tonight. How about that? How would you feel if I slit a child's throat right in front of you? I'll tell the child that you have the power to stop me, but refuse. Of course, there'll be nothing you can do to stop me from taking their faces, but they'll die thinking it's all your fault. You'll hear their cries for help and see the terror in their little eyes before I snuff them out of existence. It's all because you want to be a disrespectful whore."

No! Not the children. She tried to avert her head but couldn't move, being bound the way she was. The last thing she wanted to give him was the satisfaction of seeing her cry. How could she not? She had to convince herself that what he was doing would not be her fault. He said he was only doing this because of her, so what if he would've killed her when she was a child? Would anything be different? No, she couldn't allow him to put those thoughts into her head. Even if he did kill her as a child, he'd still be the monster he was today. Maybe even worse, because he wouldn't have the memories of his only failure hanging over his head. She was like an albatross around his neck. She seemed to be his Achilles heel, so maybe she could work that to her advantage.

When she proceeded to stare at the floor, Yates grabbed her by the hair and yanked her head back. She fell onto her back and hit her head on the concrete floor. She tried to fight back the dark spots flooding her vision by shaking her head in short bursts.

"You really are a defiant little mouse, aren't you? We need to change that. I like my victims submissive. It seems I'm going to need to break your spirit and your body. You're more resilient to pain than I imagined. Not that I'm complaining, it'll allow me to have fun with you longer. If you were weak, your body would've broken by now. I'm going to go find you a family to keep you company. I could show them all the fun games we've been playing. Maybe I can find one that has very young children, maybe even a baby. That'll make you hurt. Yes, that's what I'll do." Quickly releasing her hair, he went to the corner of the room, picked up a black bag, and moved to the door. "Anything that happens tonight is on your head. You are the reason another family is going to die." He turned and walked out.

Oh my gosh, what had she done? Her body racked with uncontrollable sobs, and she wasn't able to hold in the bile any longer. He was holding to his threat and leaving her to go find another family to murder. What if she would've only played into his games a little longer? Mary screamed his name over and over, but he didn't come back. She needed more time. She prayed he'd come back and just continue his games with her. No child could possibly withstand the things that psycho came up with. She needed to think of a way to get free, or what she would do if he didn't come back empty-handed to keep his focus on her. She couldn't stand it if someone else got hurt because she was trying to act defiant and couldn't control her mouth. Damn her temper. She knew what she had to do. She'd do something she told herself over and over again that she'd never do, but if it meant keeping him from hurting another person, she would do it. Mary was going to beg.

Chapter 20

Devon and Matthews, along with about twenty MPD and security officers, covered roughly five square blocks around the library. In his gut, he felt the library was the link. This was the only lead they had, and he hoped it would pan out. Devon needed this to work. They needed this break to find Mary, or they'd be back to square one. That meant Yates would have more time with her doing God knows what.

Who knows, maybe Yates moved on from a different place of acquisition, but Devon didn't think so. He knew killers like him. They'd keep going back to what was familiar and what worked in the past. Would he even come looking for new victims when he had Mary? *His* Mary. He was so worried about her, and every minute Yates had her, he could be doing unimaginable things to her. Devon had to think positive. Mary was smart. He had every confidence she'd find a way to stall until Devon was able to find her.

The bureau's on-call psychologist, Dr. Frederick Haskin, did a video call with the agents to consult on the findings. "After reading the case files, and what you told me Ms. Anderson has pieced together, I agree, Yates would continue to stalk other families while, in turn, also holding her against her will."

"Can you explain how you came to that conclusion?" Devon asked.

"Of course, looking back to Yates's return, it coincided with the last murder. I believed Yates was putting on a show of superiority for Mary by using the death of an innocent family to showcase his appearance back in the D.C. area. If that is, in fact, true, it is reasonable to think Yates may use a new family as another show of strength against Mary. This time, he may try to include her in the process, or use it as a way to get her to succumb to submission."

Devon didn't even try to conceal his shock. "Yes, that's exactly what he'll do. Mary is strong, and he'll need to go to extreme measures to break her." That left a small window for officers to track and apprehend Yates while he was in the act of acquiring new victims. Once Yates was in custody, as long as Mary wasn't with him, they'd be able to interrogate him and get him to release the location to where he was holding Mary. They just needed to be optimistic and patient.

Devon very much lacked patience. Positive thinking was running dry, too. Everyone was starting to think this lead was a bust. The information they compiled indicated this was the location Yates used to identify new victims may have been incorrect. It had been thirty-two hours straight of surveillance on the library with no indication Yates was going to return. They even had officers posted inside the library during closing hours.

The congressmen had to pull some strings to make that happen. The library coordinator wanted to close the library down for the foreseeable future due to the threat. Devon understood the coordinator didn't want to put civilians in harm's way. But when the congressman reached out to her, she reluctantly kept business open as usual on the promise that no civilians would be harmed, and officers would cover every inch of the library floor. For the sake of the mission, the employees were not told about the undercover officers or that there was a possible threat at the library. The coordinator handled it better than anyone expected.

The library was closing in about two hours for the night when they finally caught a break. A red Ford Focus circled the parking lot before pulling into a spot in the back. That was the first thing that threw up a red flag. This looked like the same car that circled around the block a few times last night before leaving. A person got out of the car and was wearing a hoodie, face hidden from view. Another red flag. Something was familiar about this person.

Devon radioed to Detective Miller inside the library to be on watch and to radio back to him with any information. All officers were now on their guards and would be ready to watch the new player on the board. Devon wanted to be in the library, on the front line. His chief put a halt on that, claiming Devon was too close to this to be rational if confronted by Yates. The chief wasn't wrong. Devon might rip his head off before he got the information he needed. So, for now, he'd begrudgingly remain on lookout duty.

Not even ten minutes later, the doors to the library flew open as people poured out screaming. Gunshots came from inside, echoing against the vaulted ceilings of the building.

Seconds later, another MPD officer radioed Detective Miller had Yates in custody and Yates had sustained injuries. Devon was out of his car and sprinting into the library, along with about ten other officers and security agents. Finally, some good news. Devon had to make sure he was in on the interrogation and that the congressman, or Chief Parker, didn't blackball him by taking over.

As soon as Devon and Matthews walked into the library, Matthews took off to where Yates was being detained, but Devon wanted to find Detective Miller. Yates wasn't going anywhere with the number of officers posted in the library. When Devon finally made it to the back of the library where Detective Miller was posted, he found it was a cluster of officers everywhere. They were patting each other on the backs and congratulating one another. They were acting like the case was closed, but it was far from it. This was a massive win, but Yates still had Mary, and that's what was important.

He was finally able to make his way through the swarm of people to where Miller was sitting at a table. He was staring off, not listening, as another officer was congratulating him. Every few seconds, he'd look down at his hands and the blood covering them. Devon had seen that look many times before. It was the look an officer had after not only being involved in shooting a criminal but also one who'd fought for their life.

Devon walked over to Miller and knelt in front of him. "Detective, are you all right?"

Miller looked at him with troubled eyes. "Hey, Walker. I caught him. It took me twenty years, but I finally caught Jimmy Yates."

Devon reached up and put his hand on his shoulder. "Damn right you did, Miller. You're a hero. Are you hurt? There's quite a bit of blood on you. Let's have a medic check you out."

"No, most of this is Yates's blood. He only got in a few good punches before I was able to push back and pull my weapon. He was just so close to hurting that kid. Yates really is a monster. He was going to use that kid as a shield. I couldn't let that happen. That boy was so young."

Devon nodded. Miller looked like he had been in the ring with Mike Tyson. "Why don't I take you out the back and we can get out of here? You know the drill, though, since you discharged your weapon, I need to take you to the FBI field office to debrief. I'll try to make it as quick as possible so you can get home. You might even sway me to let you shower at the station and give you some FBI sweats. You don't want your wife to freak out when she sees you."

"Yeah, that might not be a bad idea. Susie knows what I do, and she accepts it, but I try not to bring it home. Especially when I look the way I do. She likes to lecture me on how I need to be more careful."

"Let's go, Miller." They moved to the back of the library where the service door was located, only being stopped about a dozen times.

"Hey, Devon," Miller said. "I'm surprised you didn't go with your partner to where they're securing Yates. I know you have a personal stake in this."

Devon was champing at the bit to get his hands-on Yates, but that was specifically why he had to stay away for right now. "Miller, honestly, if I would have walked over there, I wouldn't have been able to control myself. The most important thing is to find out where he's holding Mary, and if I would've gotten my hands on him, I may have killed him. Matthews can handle Yates; I need to hear your story. You may have more information that can help us find Mary."

"I understand, Devon. Just so you know, I wanted to kill him with every fiber of my being. I've been a cop for a long time, and Yates was always the one that got away for me. I had him on the ground after I shot him in the arm, and I had to force myself not to shoot him between the eyes. Not only did I know it wouldn't be legal, but we need to find Mary, and I know it would be almost impossible if I killed him. He'll spend his time in court, and I'll be there for every moment to make sure he never sets foot on free land again. For as long as I live, I'll never forget the look in his eyes when he realized he was cornered. In that moment, I truly believe if he could have done anything to have been able to harm that boy, he would have. In the end, that's what gave me the motivation I needed."

Chapter 21

Chief Parker hadn't made it back to the field office yet when Devon and Miller arrived, so he told Miller to go shower and he'd put on a pot of coffee. Miller knew the deal. Even though they would try to get him out as soon as possible, he'd most likely be here all night filling out reports. There was going to be so much paperwork.

Twenty minutes later, Miller finished showering off and changed, feeling a little more optimistic. Since he was MPD and not FBI, he knew his supervisor would be waiting for him to be included in the debrief. The only reason he was giving his statement at the FBI office and not his station was because it was an official FBI case. As if on cue, Captain Alexander walked through the doors as Miller was heading to the break room to get that much needed coffee. However, he didn't make it to the break room before Captain Alexander stopped him.

Captain Alexander certainly acted like he had a few pots of coffee. "You did it, Miller. You captured Jimmy Yates. Do you realize how many officers wished they were in your shoes right now? There'll be mounds of paperwork, especially since you discharged your weapon, but you're a hero. This is going to reflect so well on the department, all because of you."

Miller shook his head. "No, Sir, I did my job. I just happened to be the one stationed in that part of the library at the time Yates entered. I'm no hero, but I'm ecstatic that the murderer will be off the streets."

Captain Alexander smiled. "Now stop being modest. You saved the day. At least you didn't kill him, though many officers may not have acted with restraint like you. Congressman Carter has been throwing a fit because his niece wasn't with him at the library. We need to run through this debrief as quickly as possible so I can get over to the hospital to question Yates. I already sent officers over to stand guard outside his hospital room. Chief Parker and Agent Walker are in the conference room waiting if you're ready."

"Yes, Sir. Let's get this over with. The quicker you're done with me, the quicker you can get to finding Ms. Anderson. That needs to be a priority."

Devon was checking his watch when Miller and his captain walked into the conference room. Chief Parker, already annoyed, wanted to be at the hospital interviewing Yates, but knew he needed to do the debriefing. Of course, Parker also sent over a handful of Agents to watch Yates and try to stop any interrogation until he could get there. It was important to get the officer's accounting to pass on to his superiors. Especially since Yates may have said something before he was shot that they'd be able to use against him. And maybe then he'd tell them where he was holding Mary.

Chief Parker stopped pacing the room when Miller and Alexander walked in. "Great, everyone is here. Miller, I hope you understand we need to make this quick. I'm going to turn on the recorder. Can you please walk us through what happened?"

Everyone in the room turned to look at Miller. He moved to sit next to the recorder and folded his hands neatly on the table. Miller looked like he'd aged a few years just from the events from tonight. Letting out a big breath, he began. "Okay, I'm ready. Tonight's surveillance started just like last night. I was patrolling the 'True Crime' section, which is where the intel in Ms. Anderson's research suggested Yates might radiate towards. The first night, some people would walk around in this section, but nothing stood out. There was nothing suspicious.

"Tonight, a family of four came in, and the teenage son was looking through the books in this section, which wasn't suspicious either, but I kept a closer watch. It was really hard not to tell the boy to leave that section. Per the intel and experience, I knew Yates would look for families with children. That alone put me on edge, because I have two children of my own. All the training in the world can't make you entirely detach from your feelings with every case. Also, the thought of confronting Yates, whose crime scenes gave me my first real life glimpse into the sadistic horrors of serial killers, was a lot to process.

"I've been watching the boy that was in this section for about an hour when someone caught my eye. The library is so brightly lit, when a person came in with a hoodie pulled down around his face, they weren't able to hide their features as well as they were attempting. I was already watching that person when the call came in over the radio to be on alert. It took only seconds for Yates to notice me watching him, watching the boy.

"From the moment my eyes met Yates, I swear someone pushed the fast-forward button on reality. Behind me I heard screaming, which I never confirmed, but assumed came from the mother. She must've noticed the knife Yates pulled out and was holding at his side. Thankfully,

I noticed him reaching for his pockets, and even the women screaming behind me didn't distract me from keeping my eyes on the danger. As soon as the screaming started, he chose that moment to run towards the boy. I barely got past the boy and pushed him behind me before Yates was on top of me. I remember yelling for the boy to run. He seemed frozen in place at the sound of his mother's screams.

"Yates tried to grab my shoulder with his left hand and, at the same time, slash the knife down with his right hand. I deflected the knife, but once the knife dropped to the ground, he turned to using his hands. He got in a few good punches before I was able to get some distance between us."

Parker was the first one to interrupt detective Miller. "Why didn't you just shoot him? It was well within your power as an officer of the law. There was an evident threat to not only your life, but to every life in that library."

"The reason I didn't immediately go for my firearm, and the disabling shot, was because I didn't want to pull my weapon until the boy, his family, and everyone else in the library were completely out of the way, and that's what allowed Yates to move in. Right away, I was thankfully able to knock the knife out of his hand, so all he had left were his fists. Once I got some distance between us, that's when I pulled my firearm and went for the disabling shot. I knew we still needed Yates for questioning, so I made sure the shot wouldn't be fatal.

"I don't think Yates was expecting me to shoot him, because once he was hit, he just froze. He had a look of confusion on his face. Like he expected to be bulletproof and couldn't believe a bullet actually hurt him. He looked at the blood dripping down his right shoulder, then over to me, and back to his shoulder. His hesitation was all I needed to be able to knock him to the ground and cuff him as the other officers made their way to my section of the library, weapons drawn, ready for a fight. And that is all that went down. It was pretty fast."

Chief Parker was already moving towards the door. "You did a great job tonight, Miller. You saved that family. Let me know if you ever want to come play with the big boys. The FBI could surely use you." He didn't even wait for a reply. "Walker, let's go," Parker yelled as he left the room.

Devon stopped for a moment before racing after his Chief. "Thanks, Miller. Because of you, one less serial killer is roaming the streets praying on innocent victims, and we'll have a better chance at finding Mary. I agree with your captain. You are a hero."

Chapter 22

The hospital was, as Devon expected, a freaking circus. As soon as he and Chief Parker stepped off the elevator and onto the locked down floor, Congressman Carter, other FBI agents, the MPD police commissioner, and angry doctors and nurses bombarded them. Devon moved aside and let Parker handle that mess.

Matthews was standing only a few feet away, motioning for Devon. He made a beeline for his partner. "Dude, where have you guys been? Parker's little security detail won't let anyone but doctors and nurses into Yates's room. And even when they go into the room, they're never alone with him. They even followed Yates to the operating room when the doctors removed the bullet and stood at the door. The doctors aren't happy about any of this. They kept yelling about how they want everyone gone. The other agents wouldn't even let the police commissioner in to see Yates. Even I would've moved to the side for her. She may be tiny, but she intimidates the hell out of me." Matthews pointed back to the chief. "Looks like she's giving Parker hell for his interference. She doesn't give a damn that he's FBI and she's city police."

"I wish we would've been able to come over with you guys. We were at the office, taking Miller's statement. I think Parker wanted to see if there would be anything to use when he interrogates Yates, and he wanted to get that information before anyone else. There was nothing useful, though. It all happened so fast, and Yates didn't even mention Mary."

"It may be a while before anyone can talk to Yates. The doctor put him under sedation at Yates's request. Apparently, he convinced a naïve doctor that he was in too much pain to function, and the doctor believed him and gave him heavy drugs. That doctor screwed up majorly. The last report I got from Scott was that Yates was completely out."

Devon's hand flexed at his side. Matthews knew in an instant that the news about the sedation pissed him off. "Man, what else can go wrong? I need Yates awake now. We need to find Mary. Just give me a minute alone with him, and I'll wake him up."

Devon made his way towards Parker, pushing people aside. His superior could be a dick at times, but he sure knew how to get things done. Parker looked irate when Devon grabbed his arm and pulled him out of the wave of people. "You better have a damn good excuse for interrupting me, Walker."

"Yes, Sir. I don't know if anyone informed you that the doctors sedated Yates at *his* request. He needs to answer questions but, because of that reckless doctor, Yates is unconscious. Mary's life hangs in the balance, and I won't be delayed any longer in questioning him. In my opinion, the best way to get everyone off your back and be the hero is to find Mary quickly." Devon knew if he played to his Chief's ego, he'd have a better chance to get what he wanted.

If this would've been any other time, the chief's change in demeanor would've been laughable. Parker straightened up, pushed his chin out, and put his hands on his hips. "You're right. We need to find the victim, and I can make that happen. Where's that doctor? He's going to explain to me why he took it upon himself to compromise my case. And he better have a damn good excuse, or Congressman Carter might push to have his license revoked. He'd have the full backing of the FBI if he decided to press charges."

Parker pushed through the nurses, grabbed the doctor by his arm, and dragged him into Yates's room and slammed the door. Devon stood outside, where he could still see Parker. Yes, the wheels were certainly in motion as Parker pointed his finger in the doctor's face, then turned and pointed to Yates. Whatever he was saying was evidently agitating the doctor, because the doctor started to yell at the chief. Hmm, that was something new. In all his years as an agent under Parker's command, he'd never seen anyone yell at him.

Parker took out his cell phone, yelled something back, then the doctor turned and walked out the door. Devon took that moment to walk into the room. "Yes, you'll do whatever I want and need or I'll take this to the media! If Ms. Anderson dies, you better damn well believe your doctors and hospital will be to blame, and under investigation so fast you–good. Good, I'm glad we could work this out, Chief to CEO. Right. Great talking to you. Bye." Parker hung up with a smug, satisfied smile. The hospital mustn't have wanted that much negative publicity.

The doctor, looking completely furious, walked back into the room with a syringe in his hand. Parker walked over and stopped the doctor before he could give Yates the injection. "What are you giving him?"

The doctor's face was white with rage. "It's something to wake the patient up. Don't you worry, I was told by the top of the hospital that I'm not allowed to do my job efficiently, and I need to cater to you. I don't know what you said to him, but I was ordered to wake this person up. It's probably useless for me to ask that you don't agitate him, isn't it?"

Parker shook his head and looked at the doctor like he was an idiot. "Don't you know who this is? This is serial killer Jimmy Yates. He kills little kids and murders entire families, but you still want to protect him? Most sane people would like to see him dead. Me included, but not before we get a chance to save his latest victim. Now wake him up!"

The doctor took a step towards Parker. "Yes, I know who this is. You don't need to be so crass. My oath means I try to do all in my power to do the best for every patient, no matter if they are a psychotic killer or not. I hope I can get him well enough to stand trial for his heinous crimes. He deserves to spend the rest of his life behind bars. That doesn't alter the care I'm sworn to provide him. If us doctors and nurses only provided care to those people that have done no harm, ninety percent of our patients would be out of luck." Parker moved aside for the doctor to give the injection. "There, he should start waking up in about fifteen minutes. I'll open the IV line so it will deliver more fluids and expedite the process." With that, the doctor left the room without another word.

A thought then came to Devon. "Hey Chief, did anyone from the agency go through his personal belongings? Maybe he had something on him that may provide any clues as to where he is holding Mary."

Chief Parker shook his head. "Not that I know of. From what I was told, no one had access to Yates but doctors and nurses. His belongings should be in the closet. Go ahead and go through them and see if there's any clue or anything that has any significance to the case. Don't forget gloves. There are some hanging on the wall."

Devon opened the closet to find the white personal belongings hospital bag. After donning gloves he found on the wall next to the bed, he started pulling items out. He soon started to lose hope for any clues to Mary's location. He did, however, find something that almost made the little bit of control he still possessed snap. It was Mary's ring. She never took it off. Yates, that bastard, must have forced it off. Devon pulled out his wallet and placed it carefully inside. He didn't want to put it on his little finger and run the possibility of losing it, or someone seeing it and taking it from him.

He knew he was breaking the chain of evidence, but he didn't care. There was a chance that he'd lose his job over taking the ring but, nothing was going to stop him from giving the ring back to Mary the moment he found her. He knew if he gave the ring to the forensics team, it would be stuck in an evidence locker for months, if not longer. It would devastate Mary not to get her ring back once this nightmare was over. He'll never forget the story behind her precious ring. And he'd never forget how emotional she got telling him that story as they sat together on the sofa, tears were rolling down her cheeks. Devon would make sure she got it back. It's her most cherished possession.

Chief Parker stepped in front of Devon, interrupting his thoughts. "I need to go get some other agents and officers so they can help question Yates when he wakes up. Can I trust you alone with him while I'm gone?"

That would've been a definite no if he didn't need Yates to answer those questions. "Yes, Sir. I won't hurt him, not yet, but I need to be completely honest. After we find Mary, all bets are off."

The chief seemed to understand. He nodded and left the room. Matthews slipped in as soon as the chief was gone. He walked over to stand next to his partner. "So, I'm guessing the chief got his way and we'll soon be able to question Yates?"

Devon's eyes never left Yates's face. One simple motion and he could end his miserable life. Just a quick flick of the wrist and he'd snap his scrawny neck. But that wouldn't help them locate Mary. "Of course. Did you ever doubt that he'd get his way on this?"

Matthews was studying his partner. He knew Walker was going through hell. "Nope. So, if it doesn't matter to you, I'm going to wait right here along with you. I'm in this with you, Walker. We're going to find Mary together."

They'd been partners long enough that Devon knew Matthews would stick to him like glue and not let Devon get in trouble if he resorted to unethical means to find Mary. Matthews knew Walker would say to hell with the law if it got in the way of finding her. On more than one occasion, Matthews needed to be Devon's conscious, and today was no different.

It was closer to twenty minutes when Yates stirred. It was evident Yates was trying to hide from coming out of sedation, but Devon never took his gaze from his face. A smile spread across Yates's lips before he could get his emotions back in check. Devon saw the minute change, and knew Yates thought he was fooling them into believing he was still under sedation. Yates probably hoped to listen to the people talking around him before they realized he was awake.

Devon wouldn't let him play his little games. He'd tell them what they needed to know, even if Devon had to beat it out of him. The reign of Yates's terror was almost over. After they found Mary, Yates would pay for his crimes. Devon motioned to Matthews, and he moved to his side next to the bed. He mouthed to Matthews, "he's awake."

Matthews mouthed back, "so it begins."

Chapter 23

"Sir," Devon announced. There were so many high officials in the room that they all turned to look at Devon. "Chief Parker," Devon corrected. "Yates is awake now."

The police commissioner leaned over Yates and turned back to Walker. "Are you sure? He looks so still. I think you're mistaken, agent. He still looks asleep."

Parker spoke up. "If Agent Walker says he's awake, then he's awake."

Everyone simultaneously moved closer to Yates, except Devon and Matthews. They stood off to the side where they could observe everyone but be out of the way.

Parker had to stop Congressman Carter from jumping in and asking questions. He knew the man was too emotional to think clearly. And he should have considered himself lucky Parker even allowed him in the room; he was a civilian, after all. With his niece being Yates's hostage, and still missing, Parker shouldn't have let the congressman anywhere near Yates.

It didn't matter that Congressman Carter had friends in high places. This was still an open FBI case. Parker was just hoping to gain an important ally by being kind and letting him in on the questioning, but he still needed everyone to keep back and let them do their jobs. Devon walked over to Congressman Carter, put a hand on his shoulder, and quietly said, "Stand over here with us. Chief Parker will get the answers we need."

Carter didn't want to move, but one look at Devon and he knew what he was talking about. He admired the drive in the young agent and knew he'd get the answers they needed to find Mary. From what Mary told him, he could see Agent Walker was infatuated with her and would move heaven and earth to find her.

Parker was trying his hardest not to lay hands on Yates. He knew he needed to act like an FBI Field officer and not do anything Yates's lawyer could use against them in court. The last thing he needed was to be the reason any charges against Yates got thrown out. And, in this day and age, lawyers could file charges on even the tiniest infractions. No, he'd get his answers without violence.

"Yates, do you know where you are?" Parker asked calmly.

Yates didn't respond or move. Unamused, the chief hit the bed railing next to Yates's head, and he flinched. "Yates, you bastard, we know you're awake. Now stop acting like a coward and open your damn eyes."

The loud noise and the blatant disrespect seemed to gain Yates's attention. His eyes shooting open, and rage covered his face. Lunging up towards the disrespectful bastard, he realized they'd handcuffed his hands to the bedside, which enraged him more. "Coward? Boy, you don't know who you're talking to. I'm the farthest thing away from being a coward. I'm the thing nightmares are made of. And I could tell you stories that'd have you wetting your pants from fear. Just wait until I get out of here, then we'll see who the coward is. I'll find everyone you've ever loved and gut them from head to toe. I'll skin them alive and make them completely unrecognizable. It would be my pleasure to add their faces to my collection. How's that for being a coward?"

"Listen," the chief interrupted, unfazed by Yates's little tirade. "You know you're caught and will be going to jail for the rest of your life. You'll never be able to harm another soul ever again. Now the only thing that can help you right now is for you to tell me where you are holding Ms. Anderson. If you tell us right now, we'll put in a good word with the DA."

A menacing laugh escaped his lips. "A good word. That doesn't mean crap to me. Will this good word stop me from being put on death row? No, it will not. So why would I tell you where I have my little plaything? Who's to say she's still alive? She could be rotting away in a shallow grave on the side of the highway somewhere. Maybe I left the pieces of her body scattered in the woods for the creatures of the night to feast on. She could be dissolving in a vat of acid right this minute. Maybe her face is already where it belongs, right next to her parents. No matter what I did with her, you'll never find her. Knowing you could spend the rest of your lives looking for her and knowing the ones she's bewitched into loving her will never find closure. That's what'll give me more satisfaction than whatever your 'good words' with the DA ever could."

Matthews grabbed hold of Walker's arm as he moved towards Yates. He'd never seen that look on Walker's face before. It was a look of rage mixed with panic. Matthews didn't believe Yates killed Mary yet, but Walker couldn't stand hearing what Yates had possibly done to her. "No, Walker. Don't interrupt. The bastard's just trying to get Parker riled. If he's saying this stuff to the chief to gain a rise, what do you think he'd say to you? Let Parker see what he can get out of him." He whispered into his friend's ear.

"You are a sick son of a bitch, but I think you're scared." Parker stated, once again ignoring Yates's comments. "Your cooperation will not keep you off death row, but we may be able to make a deal to make your stay while you wait for the needle a little more secure. Most inmates don't take kindly to people that kill innocent children. How do you think they'll feel about a person who kills babies too? Let me tell you, if you don't take my advice, I'll make sure you get released into the general population section of the worst prison you can imagine. If that happens, I project you won't last twenty-four hours. And if there is anyone in the prison that doesn't know your past, which is very unlikely, I'll ask the guards to casually mention it to some inmates. And just to let you know, gossip travels at the speed of light in the prison system. Once they find out what you did to the children, you wouldn't make it to bedtime. They won't kill you easily; they'd make you suffer for a long, long time. I also don't think the guards would be in such a hurry to stop them, either. They'd probably just turn their backs and let the situation play out before breaking it up. You know, for their own safety. So, if you tell us where Ms. Anderson is, we can keep you in isolation. Do we have an understanding?"

Yates feigned consideration for the bargain. But then he gave an evil grin. "No, I don't think we have a deal. That little bitch has made my life miserable for over twenty years. I'll die happy knowing that she suffered until her last breath, and that you'll never find her body to put her to rest. Not that there will be much left of her body to find. I think

I'll just sit here, close my eyes, and visualize all the torment she's going through right now, at this very moment."

Parker's eyebrow rose. "So, she's still alive?"

Yates laughed. "Of course she is. Well, at least she was when I left her. I'm not so sure how long she will last. Did you think I'd end her torture and kill her quickly? I knew when I went to the library to pick out the next victim that I needed to put a safeguard in place in case I wasn't able to return to her. Her agony won't end just because you caught me. No, Sir. You most certainly extended her suffering. With how I left her, she will be in anguish for a long time, and I'll enjoy thinking about it every moment. Now, not only will she die slowly from what I've already done to her, but she'll also starve to death. Unless you let me go back to her, no one will be there to feed your little mouse." He turned to look at Devon right in the eyes, knowing he was there the entire time. "Mr. Walker. Why are you hiding all the way in the back? Come up here and join me. I feel that over the last few weeks, I've come to know you quite well."

Devon slowly made his way up to the bed, all eyes now on him. Matthews followed him, keeping right next to him, in case he needed to stop Devon from lunging and choking the life out of Yates. He had a foreboding feeling about what Yates was going to say to his partner, and he knew Devon's temper.

"Mr. Walker, at last we meet. I have been watching you and Ms. Anderson for weeks now. It was disgusting to watch, and very unprofessional. You two have become quite the little couple. Intimately locked away in her apartment, thinking you had her tucked away and safe. That's why this is going to be so much fun. I can see by your expression that you'd like nothing more than to hurt me, probably in the same ways

I hurt your little girlfriend. Isn't that correct? More than that, I bet you are champing at the bit to hear about Ms. Anderson. Do you want me to tell you what I have been doing to the lovely mouse? Do you want me to tell you how I've made her scream, how I've made her bleed? Oh, of course you do. That's why you are all here, surrounding my bed."

It took all Devon's strength not to reach over and snuff the life out of the bastard. It helped that Matthews had an iron strong grip on his right arm. Gritting his teeth, he took a deep breath before opening his mouth. "You know I don't want to hear what you've done to Mary. I'd rather you tell me where she is."

The corners of his eyes crinkled as he focused on Devon's face. "Now that wouldn't be any fun. But just to make you feel a little better, she's not alone. There are lots of other things down there with her, and they want to play with her as much as I did, maybe more. Although they may not be as gentle."

Devon was icy with panic. Things? What did he mean? Down there? She must be underground. He felt Matthews place his other hand on his left shoulder and knew it was either for support or to stop him from attacking the psychopath. Shaking a little, Matthews dropped both hands, but stayed close.

"Now, are you going to let me tell you a story? If you pay attention, maybe I'll throw in some meager clues as to where you can find your precious Ms. Anderson. So, listen closely to every word. I'm going to start by telling you all about the fun we've been having. I'll tell you the story about my time with Ms. Anderson, cut by tiny cut."

Devon's head felt like it was on fire. With every word that came out of Yates's mouth, it was like a spike being driven into his brain. This man before him had kidnapped and done unspeakable things to the woman he loved very much. It took all his willpower not to double over in agony. He felt a reassuring hand quickly touch his shoulder to let him know someone was close and knew without looking that it was still Matthews at his side. Matthews had a bad feeling that if they didn't find Mary safe, Walker would tear Yates limb from limb and there'd be nothing anyone could do to stop him.

"Let's see, where to begin, where to begin?" Yates mocked. "Playing with sweet Mary has been so much fun. I've been planning for the moment I'd finally gotten my hands on her for years. I wanted to make our time together special, so I looked to our ancestors of yore. They were much more brutal than the weaklings of today. Why they banned such effective punishments, I'll never understand." Looking around the room, he saw a mixture of looks of horror and people wanting to vomit. He was going to have some fun.

"The first game we played was a page straight out of the bible. Stoning. I decided that Mary's offense was witchcraft, so I was well inside my biblical rights to see her stoned. However, I didn't take it all the way and kill her. No, no. Even though a few times I came very close. I learned quickly to stay away from hitting her in the head. She's mighty weak, and I wanted her awake for our games. We had lots more fun after that. The next game we played was a little more modern. I tried to freeze her to death. You know what? That little bitch stood her own and wouldn't die. She was very inconveniencing, so I decided I needed to get a little more creative."

Terror sealed Devon's throat as he took a single step forward before being stopped. Matthews grabbed hold of one of Devon's arms, and Chief Parker grabbed the other. Both could see the pain in his eyes, and although they wouldn't blame him for killing Yates, they still needed him alive. The last thing Matthews wanted to do was watch his partner get arrested for murder. Even though the world would be a better place without Yates, the law was still the law.

"Oh, Mr. Walker, I can see you're entertained and want to hear more. Please, let me oblige." Yates continued, "I really did think about killing her. I could've actually frozen her to death, but I got bored with how long it was taking her to die. The next two games we played were much more fun and would've made your CIA proud. Maybe you should take notes and send them to them. We started with a little game called dry boarding. For those of you that are looking at me with blank stares, I'll tell you what that is. I took a plastic bag, shoved it over the bitch's head, and held it there till she almost suffocated to death. Of course, her hands were bound, so it was fun watching her pull and thrash against the binds, trying to reach for the bag. Oh, we had fun with this one. We played this for quite a few hours. I finally had to stop because I went a little far and thought I had actually killed her. I couldn't have that happen; we wouldn't be able to play any more games if she died. I decided I wasn't done with her. She didn't suffer enough to make up for all the torment she's put me through over the years. We still had a long way to go."

Congressman Carter's composure finally snapped. He wasn't able to stand there and listen to this scumbag describe all the ways he hurt his niece. Mary was strong, and would hold out as long as she could, but dread had been growing inside Robert with every word from Yates. Finally, his panic increased so much it spilled out and he started shouting obscenities at Yates as he tried to push through the agents. Alex, his head of security, grabbed him around the torso and restrained him. "No,

Sir," is all the guard said, and the congressman stopped struggling, but stiff with pain.

Yates winked at the security guard, Alex. "Since I was so rudely interrupted, can someone remind me where I was in my story?" Looking around the room, not one person answered. They all maintained their stone-cold composure for now.

Snapping his fingers enthusiastically, he continued. "Oh yes, I remember now. Onto the next game. Have any of you heard a person scream with such fear and torment in their voices that it affected you all the way to your core, deep to your soul? It's such an amazing sound. I, for one, could listen to that to fall asleep. Mary didn't like it as much. I played a loop of a teenage girl screaming and begging for her life that I'd recorded during one of my cleanses for her. I made her listen to the recording for about six hours while I ran some errands. Mary had the pleasure of listening to my handiwork. When I came back, she was curled into herself like a baby. It was quite pathetic. I had to kick her a few times to get her to stop sobbing and pay attention to me again. I was so ecstatic it had the results I was hoping for. Finally, I'd mentally broken her. Now, I needed to break her physically, which is the easy part. So, I moved on to the last and most fun game of all. I wanted to see if I could complete lingchi."

Matthews knew what that meant and gripped both Devon's arms so tight it became extremely painful. Devon tried to shake off the restraint, but Matthews wouldn't budge, and pulled Devon both back and into his own.

"Are you all loving my storytelling so far? The best is yet to come. Do any of you smart government people know what lingchi is? No? No takers? Touchy crowd. It is death by a thousand cuts."

Devons became disoriented at what he had just said. Pain crashed through every fiber of his body. If it wasn't for Matthews and his painful grip on his arms, his knees would have given out and he would've fallen to the ground. He vaguely felt his friend lean in, but heard him whisper, "be strong, Mary needs you." That was the reasoning he needed to hold on to. Mary was still alive, and he needed to keep a clear head, no matter what.

"Playing with my new knife was fun. At first, she wouldn't even make a sound. It wouldn't be fun if she wouldn't react to my games. So I stabbed her instead. I couldn't do that too many times, though, or I'd never make it to a thousand. So I only stabbed her when she refused to cry out with my little cuts." He looked around the room, locking onto her uncle. "Congressman, you should be proud of your niece. You raised her to be strong. Maybe a little too strong, because it made me mad, so I cut her even more. A bit deeper every time she showed me defiance. I'm not sure how many cuts I inflicted on the little mouse before I left, but I know she was more red than white. Since her lips were blue from near hypothermia, she was very patriotic looking. Red, white, and blue." He laughed hysterically.

Devon fought to keep down the bile rising in his throat. It was almost impossible to listen to Yates explain every heinous torture he executed on Mary. God, what she had to have been going through; what she was still going through. She had to be terrified, but he felt a little pride knowing she was frustrating Yates beyond reason with her strength. Then, as Yates continued talking, Devon's heart dropped.

"So, like I was saying, she is a little mouse, so she may as well die of her own kind. Since I'm no longer with her, I can't protect her. Can anyone in this room tell me how to make a rat go into a frenzy?" He looked around the room, but no one spoke up. Not that he expected anyone to. "Fine. It's no fun that none of you want to play along, so I'll tell you. Blood. Blood makes rats utterly fanatic. So, what do you think they'll do when they smell all the blood seeping from Ms. Anderson? Just think about it. The rats catch the scent of blood coming from her cuts, and they'll run along the sewer pipes, drawn to their next meal. They won't need to run far to find her, and she's staked out nice and pretty, so she won't be able to fend them off. So hopefully you've been listening closely. It's the only way you have a chance to get to her before the rats do. I'll gain entertainment thinking of you all scurrying around, to no avail."

The room was so silent, the sound of a pin dropping would have been like a bomb exploding. How could he have put Mary through all that and she still survived? What a sadistic bastard. To make the entire situation even worse, if that was possible, Yates started singing. He was freaking singing, and to the tune of 'Mary Had a Little Lamb'.

"Mary is surrounded by big fat rats, big fat rats, big fat rats. Mary is surrounded by big fat rats and they're going to eat her up. Happy hunting." He burst into maniacal laughter.

Chapter 24

Devon couldn't take any more. He stormed out of the room and over to the elevator. Matthews and Parker were right behind him. Both men knew better than to stop Devon. One look in his eyes would tell anyone he'd kill the next person who got in his way.

As soon as the three were in the elevator, Devon spoke up. Despair radiated with every word. "We've got to find her." His voice cracked. "She's without a doubt terrified right this instant. How could someone do those things to another human being? I've met my share of sickos, but Yates is by far the most malicious." He punched the wall of the elevator.

Matthews was the only one with a cool head. Like Devon, he, too, had grown to care for Mary in the last few weeks. The only reason he could keep cool was because he had to be the voice of reason for his partner. "Listen, Walker. I recorded that conversation; we'll identify the meanings of his hints. He thinks he's so smart, but we're smarter. Let's head back to the office and we'll listen to the recording on the way and see what we can piece together."

Devon wanted to go back into the hospital room and bash Yates's head against the wall until he told him where he was keeping Mary. It was vital for them to find her soon if everything he told them was true. Devon knew exactly how rats reacted to blood. He'd seen them at many crime scenes, eating the bodies of the recently deceased. Mary wouldn't suffer that fate; they'd find her. Please, let them find her.

Mary kept going in and out of consciousness. Yates had gone a bit crazy on the cuts before he left her for the last time. At least he didn't turn the screaming back on before he left. She needed to remember not to get him too upset. It was hard. She wanted to kill him with her bare hands for the things he said about her parents. She was fighting the darkness when she thought she heard something by the door. Mary wasn't sure how long she was unconscious, but she was hoping it wasn't long enough for him to be back already. She wasn't ready for the torture to continue, but most of all, she was worried he'd succeed at fulfilling his promise and found a family to murder. Though she was strong willed– her aunt and uncle had drilled that into her head for years and she knew it was true–she also knew she couldn't handle Yates harming another family because of her. Or anyone. Especially a child. She would do anything to save a child from this psychopath. Anything.

Though she worried about Yates returning and who he might bring with him, there was something far more important to worry about. Mary looked toward the door, finally realizing what was making the scratching noise she'd been hearing. *Rats*. Her mouth went dry. She shook with fear, and bile clawed up her throat. Rats, according to everything she'd read and studied through college, were brutal. Studies showed rats have a real thirst for blood. In an experiment, researchers gave them an array of different foods and liquids to consume in a twenty-four-hour period. The blood that was supplied as an option was equivalent to four times the amount of food they would consume in a day, and the rats drank every drop. At the time of the study, scientists were still unsure of what attracted them to the blood. All Mary knew was that there was lots of blood, her blood, surrounding her on the floor, and on her clothes, and the rats smelled it.

With her hands and feet tied on the floor, she couldn't stand up to get away from the rats if they moved closer. She had to keep them from coming too close. She knew how to get out of plastic zip tie cuffs by using her shoestrings as a makeshift saw and wondered if the rope would work the same way. It couldn't hurt to try. It was either that, or she could give up. But Mary wasn't a quitter, and she would not give Yates the satisfaction of her surrender, not if she could help it.

Sleep deprivation and trauma were wreaking havoc on her problem-solving skills. She'd practiced over and again on how to use shoe strings to break out of zip ties, but that was with unbound feet, and not rope. She knew she could alter that training, but how? Time was ticking by when she decided to just play it by ear. Her hands and feet were bound by thick rope to a loop in the ground. She had enough wiggle room to reach her shoestrings, and after moving her wrists around, she felt she'd be able to make small sawing motions. It was worth a shot. Untying her laces, she tied two ends together, making sure one part of the wrist binding was underneath. Very slowly, she began moving her wrists side to side like a hacksaw, hoping to fray the rope one thread at a time.

After working on the rope for a while, a few strands were finally fraying. It was going to take ample more work, but Mary was determined to break free from her bonds. The rats, on the other hand, were determined to make a meal out of her. While she was concentrating on the ropes, one brave rat got a good bite in on her right side. She didn't even hear the little bugger moving closer, but, dang; she felt him.

She found most of them would scurry off when she made a sudden movement, or yelled at them, but not this one. This rat was determined to come back. She started to feel optimistic about her progress, but then the shoestring broke. She had one more to use, but if that broke, she would be stuck. Every time she made a sawing movement, the cuts on her arms and legs seeped a little more blood, and started a frenzy with a few of the rats, eager to bite into her again.

She paused for a moment, frustrated and anxious to break free. She couldn't decide if she should slow down or go faster, risking the other shoestring breaking like the one before. Taking advantage of the moment, the rat ran up and got another bite in. She fought her rising panic and urge to speed up, and knew one wrong move and she'd be stuck and unable to escape. Even in a near state of complete panic, she slowed down. If she took her time and kept a steady pace, she'd be able to keep an eye on the rats a little better. She'd be lucky if she didn't get rabies. She'd seen an animal suffer with rabies, and she'd seen a human suffer with rabies, and that wasn't how she'd want to die.

Devon, Matthews, and Chief Parker went to Mary's house instead of the field office, and they made it in record time. Devon broke almost every traffic law on his way there, but he didn't care. Matthews sent a message to the congressman letting him know where they were heading and suggested that he and his security team head to his niece's apartment. Devon didn't want people to get in his way, but the more eyes and ears, the better. Anything to help find Mary as quickly as possible.

When Congressman Carter, followed by four of his security team, walked into his niece's apartment, the recording of everything Yates said to them in the hospital room was playing on repeat over the speaker system. "What do you got, Walker? Please tell me you have something."

Motioning Carter to his side, Devon rushed through, explaining the information they put together. "We know from the recording Mary is either in the sewer or near sewer pipes. Rats are more often underground than above. We also know that it wouldn't take Yates long to get to the library. He was hunting for a new family, and he wouldn't want to travel very far with them, or leave Mary for an extended period of time, so that gave us an idea of a general perimeter."

Matthews pulled out a pipeline map, one of the other agents from the sewer utility company acquired. He tacked it up on the wall for everyone to see. Devon stepped up to the map and took the lead. "I hate to assume, but in this case, we need to. So, let's assume it took him a max of fifteen minutes to leave Mary and make it to the library. We are looking at about a five-mile radius. Yes, this doesn't seem like a lot, but we are just outside the city so traffic time is still bad. This map shows all the sewer lines for this suburb and the ones surrounding the library. If you notice, Mary's childhood house is almost dead center in this radius. So, I'm pretty confident we are on the right track."

He pointed to the dots on the map. "These are the locations of manholes that are next to underground storage areas that would be large enough to hold a person." He pointed to squares on the map. "And these are service stations where city workers go down and work on pipes and electronics. This is where I feel he would hold Mary. He'd need ample room to secure her and have room for torture." It hurt him to say torture in relation to Mary, but he had to be Agent Walker right now. Agent Walker was ruthless and unstoppable. That's what Mary needed him to be, someone that would stop at nothing. Someone with a personal stake in her safety. Yates was too arrogant and thought himself brilliant. Devon would prove him wrong. If he didn't play his clue game when he was boasting, they may never have gained any leads.

"Chief Parker, how many agents do you think you can gather in the next ten minutes?" Devon asked.

Chief Parker was already pulling out his phone. "The whole field office. We have twenty agents, and every one of them is already on standby."

Congressman Carter spoke up, "We have four guys here and I can pull the rest on my staff. I can provide ten in all. I'll call the MPD commissioner and get her guys as well. You have the plan. Just tell me what you need to implement it and find my niece. You'll get anything you need."

For once, Chief Parker wasn't trying to take the spotlight. He'd have realized by now that Walker wasn't going to sit on the sidelines on this one or be content to simply take orders.

Devon waved his hands in the air to pull everyone's attention and gather them closer. "Okay, here's what we need to do. We need to break into two-man teams, all with communications. On my mark, we'll each hit a different manhole that is close to a service port. Once everyone checks in, if needed, we move to the next set of points. It's important that we all strike at the same time. I doubt Yates would have a partner, but we can't take any chances. He's not shown any indications in the past of having an accomplice, but everyone needs to be on the lookout for booby-traps. A desperate man is unpredictable. We'll need fifty-two officers in two-man teams. There are one-hundred and four entry points, so each team will take four points close to each other. Congressman Carter, see if the MPD can spare twenty-two officers. We need to move out in twenty minutes and meet at a centralized command center. There is a post office with a large parking lot within our radius. Let's send out the message to have all involved meet there now. Once everyone is checked in, Matthews will give each group the addresses for their checkpoints."

Congressman Carter came through for them, and more. They needed fifty-two officers and ended up with sixty for their mission. Plus Yates's room at the hospital was crowded with armed officers. The congressman called in some favors from other political officials, and they donated their security teams. It was five minutes until two a.m., and that was the hit time. Everyone was doing their radio checks and stood ready to go. Even though it was Devon's plan to all hit at the same time, it was almost impossible for him to wait. He wanted to get down there and start searching.

Mary didn't know how much more she could take. The rope binding her wrists was threading, but not fast enough. Yates had been gone a long time, and Mary knew she was running out of time. A single rat was no longer running out of reach when she lunged towards them. He'd bite her side, back, arms, legs, and feet. She could barely move to continue sawing at the rope with the constant interruption from the vermin. Maybe if she stopped, she would pass out and not feel the pain anymore.

She tried to push that thought from her mind. She didn't want to give Yates the satisfaction of proving she wasn't as strong as she knew she was, as she had to be to survive. On the other hand, she'd finally be able to see her parents again. Oh, how she missed them. Yates would've killed her parents even if they told him where she was hiding, but they didn't, and that made their suffering that much worse. Their suffering was her fault, and she wouldn't let it be in vain.

She owed it to her parents, and to all his other victims, to stay strong and make sure they brought Yates to justice. And she wouldn't be able to achieve that by giving up. And what about Devon? In the short time she'd known him, she was confident he wouldn't give up looking for her. Even if it was only out of obligation, though she hoped that wasn't the only reason.

He said he wanted to talk the night she was abducted, and she was hoping it was to tell her he cared for her. Mary needed to keep pushing on for him. She needed more time with him. She didn't want him to think he had failed her, so she needed to stay alive. Knowing how Devon was, Mary knew if she didn't make it out, he'd blame himself for Yates getting his hands on her.

She'd continue to work on this rope, one stroke at a time, but she also needed to worry about that damn rat. She'd already lost so much blood, and every time the rat took another bite, her vision blurred. One step at a time, one more slide of the shoestring against the rope. It was all she could do. Leaning over, she focused on the movements of the fraying rope. She would make it. She had to make it.

Chapter 25

Matthews took over the radio. Once they descended into the sewer system, he knew his partner wouldn't be worried about communicating with the rest of the team. Walker would have tunnel vision, and Mary was on the other end. He prayed they'd get lucky. He needed Walker to get a win. Matthews suggested that he and Walker take the service opening closest to Mary's childhood home. He had a feeling about it.

The library was also exceptionally close to her childhood home. It could've been a coincidence, but Devon didn't think so. He'd worked with psychopaths before, and they tend to cling to the sentimental. It was usually their downfall and how they got caught. And Matthews didn't believe in coincidences. Especially when there were just too many with this case.

At exactly two a.m., Matthews gave the signal to move. All teams went radio silent and moved on to their identified targets. If all went according to plan, within ten minutes, every team would be at their marks and checking in with their status. Chief Parker and Congressman Carter were above ground, assisting with coordinating all the teams.

The sewer system was as Devon imagined it. They would have been completely lost if not for the detailed blueprints they received from the city. Pulling out his flashlight, he saw a network of different pipelines. The only place to walk, not submerged in questionable water, was a small concrete walkway against the wall that was no more than twelve inches wide. He checked his compass to make sure they were heading in the right direction. The last thing they wanted to do was get lost, which would be very easy to do.

Matthews's boots scraped the floor behind him as he made a left turn and into complete darkness. The sounds of scurrying feet made his heart pound. Devon knew there were going to be rats and other animals in the sewer, but he hoped Mary was a place where they couldn't reach her. That hope was fastly diminishing as his flashlight caught movement up ahead and dozens of glowing red eyes. He knew in an instant they needed to move faster.

Mary was finally making headway. Another thread of the rope broke. She only had two more to go, then she would be free. Suddenly, her eyes watered and the hairs on the back of her neck bristled. Something was moving outside the door. Was Yates back? Had he been successful and kidnapped another family? Slowly, the door handle turned. Mary tried to scream. If there was another family with him, maybe they would fight harder to get away, but nothing came out. Her mouth was as dry and barren as a desert, and what came out was little more than a croak. She breathed in and out, but no air seemed to enter her lungs. She suddenly felt starved for air and her imagination ran wild.

The door handle jiggled again. Maybe it wasn't Yates, or maybe Yates sent someone else down here to get her. Her heart pounded so hard it sounded like water was rushing through her head, and everything around her started to go dark.

Matthews knelt down and was digging in his bag to pull out his lock picking tools. "Give me two seconds and I'll have this door open."

"We don't have two seconds." Devon said. He grabbed Matthews by the arm, pulling him to his feet. "Move aside. I'll get the door open." It was an old door, already rusting around the hinges. With one swift kick, the door splintered open. The sight before him brought him to his knees. Mary, bloody, tied to the floor, and dozens of rats scattering away from her.

"Mary," His voice cracked. Matthews's hands scooped under his arms, helping him up off his knees. He couldn't take his eyes off Mary. Matthews was already on the radio, letting everyone know they'd found her and started giving the location.

As soon as Mary saw Devon, every feeling, every fear she'd been holding in came crashing out at the speed of light. Her eyes flooded with tears, and her heart hammered in her chest with the realization she was safe. She knew they'd be looking for her, but her hope of rescue had lessened with each passing hour, and she'd desperately tried for so long to escape on her own. Her hands were numb from sawing at the rope around her hands. But he was here. And if he was here, where was Yates? What about the family he was bragging about killing? In a split second, she worried what would happen to Devon and Matthews if Yates came back. At least they had each other to watch one another's backs.

Devon was worried about how truly scared Mary looked. "Mary? Mary, it's Devon and Matthews." He wanted to make sure she knew who it was as he slowly moved towards her with his hands out in front of him. He wanted to get her untied as quickly as possible. Having worked with trauma victims in the past, he knew he needed to take it easy with her. Devon glanced back at Matthews and nodded his head. Having worked together so long, Matthews knew what he was asking. Devon moved to Mary's side and continued to talk to her. He wanted to distract her when Matthews pulled out his knife to cut the rope. After looking her over, and seeing what Yates had done, he wouldn't blame her if she never touched a knife another day in her life.

While Yates had explained everything he'd done to Mary, it was one hundred percent worse seeing it in person. Just looking at her, he was thankful she'd survived. She'd had enough trauma in her life. Nobody deserves something like this happening to them. Now all he wanted to do was get her to the hospital and spend the rest of his life keeping her safe and showering her with nothing but love.

"Mary, you're safe now. Yates won't ever touch you again. We have him. He'll be going to jail for the rest of his life." Devon explained, keeping her attention on him. She let out a small sob, then leaned into him, putting her head on his shoulder. Matthews made quick work cutting through the remainder of the rope around her hands and feet.

The moment she was free, after conducting a quick examination of her injuries, Devon scooped her up into his arms. Mary winced. "I'm sorry, sweetheart. We need to get you out of here and to the hospital. You're going to be fine. There are lots of people waiting to see you, Mary." Leaning down, he kissed her forehead. It was then he noticed she was shaking. He turned to Matthews. "Ambulance?"

Matthews nodded. "Already on its way, and should be here by the time we get back up. Parker is going to send more men down here in case we need assistance." Matthews took off his jacket, gently placing it over Mary. "Don't worry about the shaking, man. Now that the adrenaline is starting to wane from her, she's going to start feeling the cold and everything she went through. Once we get her topside, the paramedics will take care of her."

Devon was grateful he had a friend like him. They were like an old married couple. They can finish each other's sentences, and even their thoughts. Neither one ever had to wonder if the other had their back.

They were slowly moving back to the manhole where they entered the sewer. Devon was trying to move carefully to not jar Mary and cause her more pain or fall into the dirty water. With the cuts all over her body, falling into the water would certainly lead to more infection.

For what Yates did to her, he wanted to flay the bastard alive, then let the rats come after *him*. It was hard to determine where exactly the blood was coming from. She was completely covered in cuts, and her clothes were soaked and tattered. Carrying Mary up the ladder to the street was the hard part, but he wouldn't let anyone else help him but Matthews. He never wanted to let her go.

As soon as they stepped up onto the street, Congressman Carter came running over. "Oh, sweet Mary. You are going to be okay, baby girl. You're safe now."

He gently laid his hand on Mary's cheek, and she leaned into it. Tears were flowing down his cheeks. It was a side of the congressman Devon had never seen before. He'd only seen the tough as nails chew you up and spit you out, politician. This was the loving uncle who'd raised Mary and loved her like his own daughter. He was grateful for this man. It was because of his and his wife's influence that Mary turned out to be the amazing woman she was today. After the trauma she experienced as a child, her aunt and uncle gave her the love she needed to succeed in life, to survive.

The paramedics ran over with a gurney, and Devon gently laid her down. He stepped back to allow them to work, but he wasn't going to let her out of his sight. The lead paramedic had questions, and Devon pulled Congressman Carter over so he could be included. "We're going to take Ms. Anderson to the hospital, but is there any medical information we should know about before we move her?"

Congressman Carter spoke first. "She has no known allergies, so please give her whatever she needs."

The paramedic nodded and turned to Devon. "Do you have any information you can add since you are the one that found Ms. Anderson? Can you tell me any information about her injuries?"

Devon nodded. "She hasn't spoken since we found her about ten minutes ago. She just looks around with a blank stare and cries. I ran my hands around her body, and I don't think she has any broken bones. I don't think any damage was done to the bones in her neck either since she was moving it around, but it's completely covered with bruises, so I didn't want to probe too much. She has cuts and stab wounds all over her body, but with all the blood, I can't be one hundred percent sure how bad they are. I didn't get into an in-depth examination in the sewer. I just wanted to get her out of there and up here to you guys. From the information that was given to us by her abductor, she's been stoned, brought close to hypothermia, suffocated, surrounded by loud noises, cut and stabbed. Rats have also bitten her a bunch of times. There could be more, but that's what we know right now."

207

One of the other paramedics yelled they were ready to roll. "Okay, got it. Are either of you riding with us?" Both said yes at the same time. The paramedic looked like he wanted to argue, but one look from Devon made him change his mind.

Devon glanced over at Matthews, Parker, and Miller getting into an FBI SUV. They'd be following them to the hospital. Once they reached the hospital, Mary was whisked away to a room to be examined. The emergency room nurse was not happy with the two men trying to strong arm her into letting them into the room, but when she explained she would need to remove Mary's clothes to examine the cuts and bites, both Devon and Carter conceded.

They were not alone in the waiting room for long. Congressman Carter's lead security agent, Alex, rushed home at the congressman's orders and picked up Mary's aunt. Moments later, Matthews, Parker, Miller, and almost the rest of the sixty law enforcement officials showed up and amassed in the waiting room and settled in to wait for an update. It was an amazing show of support. Mary's aunt went officer by officer, giving each one a big hug and her gratitude. It was a heartfelt show of respect for these officers.

It seemed like forever before the doctor came out to give an update. Of course, she was only able to talk to Carter and his wife, as they were the next of kin. Out of respect, the Carter's pulled Devon over and told the doctor that anything she told them, Devon needed to be included on.

Obliging, the doctor explained, "Mary is stable right now, but it's going to be a long road to recovery, but the important thing that I want to stress is that she will recover. Mary was in hypovolemic shock when she was brought in tonight. The shock was due to blood loss and dehydration. Hypovolemic shock is where the heart is unable to pump enough blood to the body. We are treating this now, and she is already showing reassuring signs.

"The part I'm worried about is the mental trauma Mary endured. The physical trauma was almost two-hundred nasty cuts, bruised ribs, a contusion to the back of her head, damage to her windpipe, loss of blood, and of course, all the rodent bites. All of those we are treating. We are giving her some blood and administering antibiotics. Because of the rodent bites, we also gave her the first dose of the rabies vaccine.

"Whoever's caring for her when she leaves here will need to make sure she receives the other three doses. She will need them in three, seven, and fourteen days. I'll make sure that information is in the discharge papers. If she misses those shots, there could be life-threatening damage.

"The cat-scan of her head was promising. It didn't show any bleeding or punctures. The ribs will hurt for a few weeks, but if they were broken, it would have taken much longer to heal. I'd estimate about three months until Mary is feeling like her old self again, physically." The doctor paused a moment, then sighed. "Now, about the mental trauma she endured. None of us can imagine what Mary went through while she was kidnapped. From what I understand, Mary was captive for over sixty hours. With the amount of physical trauma she presents, it proves he did a lot of damage in a short time.

"Mary hasn't spoken to me or any of the nurses. This isn't much of a concern right now due to the damage to her windpipe and her shock. However, if it continues, that will be a reason for concern. Some trauma victims withdraw into places in the mind we can't follow, and don't come out until they are ready to. We've notified the hospital psychologist and he'll be meeting with Mary as soon as she wakes up. We gave her something to help her sleep. I doubt she got any rest in the last few days. What she needs right now is rest.

"I want to keep her for at least twenty-four hours for observation. Depending on what the psychologist says, you'll be able to take her home the day after tomorrow. She'll need twenty-four-hour care for a few days, as she shouldn't be alone during this time. A social worker will be by before discharge to talk to you about your options. I can take you three back now to her room. You can't stay long, visiting hours are almost over, and as I said, she needs rest. Leave all your information with the nurse, and I'll be in touch after I get a report from the psychologist."

When Devon walked into Mary's room, his heart instantly ached. Mary was wrapped up head to toe, resembling a mummy. She was hooked up to so many machines. She had electrodes on her forehead, and blood and IV fluids dripping away. The only thing that made him feel minutely better was the nice, steady sound of her heartbeat on the monitor. He needed to remember what the doctor said. She will recover. Repeating it to himself didn't make the hurt any less painful.

Mary's aunt rushed over to her side and cried again as she grabbed Mary's hand. She turned and looked at her husband, "Please tell me the person responsible will pay for what they did to our baby girl?"

Carter walked over, put his hand on his wife's shoulder, and turned to look at Devon. He was talking to him as much as he was to his wife. "Oh, trust me, he'll pay. We'll do everything in our power to see that he gets the needle. He'll never be free to do this to another person again. I'll make sure I'm present for every step of his trial."

The congressman and his wife sat on either side of Mary, each holding a hand. Devon leaned against the wall, but wouldn't take his gaze from her face. He never should've let Mary leave the other day, orders or not. None of this would've happened if he'd stayed with her and kept her locked up. No, that wasn't true. Yates would've bided his time until he had the opportunity to strike. He said he'd been watching them, so could get close without being noticed. He had to have installed cameras somewhere, but the tech team didn't find anything in her apartment. Nor did they find any listening devices.

The cameras must have been located outside the apartment. He knew Mary wouldn't have been safe as long as Yates was free. And this was the last way he wanted Yates to be apprehended, but it was over. Well, almost over. The important thing was that Mary's safe and Yates was in federal custody. Any jury in their right minds would convict Yates on all charges and seal his fate to the death penalty. Since Yates wouldn't be charged with the death penalty in D.C., and this was a federal case, Devon would suggest to Parker they coordinate with the Virginia FBI field office, so the death penalty would be a definite possibility. Yates committed a string of murders in Virginia, so that the state can claim jurisdiction.

Chapter 26

About an hour later, Chief Parker came in to pull Devon from the room. "I have some information on Yates that you need to be made of. Later today he's being moved to a supermax facility to recover. He's no longer going to stay at the hospital. Two of our agents already had to intercede with family members of his victims trying to gain access to his locked down floor.

"I want to thank you, Agent Walker. When a case crosses with a personal life, more seasoned agents lose their training and wits. I threw you into this case as a bodyguard, and in the beginning, you resented it. I hope you now see that I didn't do it as a punishment, but for the sake of Ms. Anderson. Anyone with eyes can see how you look at her. Just don't let it blind you to your job. We're nowhere near done with Yates yet. We need to finish all the paperwork, cross the T's and dot the I's, and make sure this case is ironclad. I can't stress enough how we need to make sure none of our actions give the defense a reason to question them and absolutely no reason to throw out a charge because of negligence on our part.

"I need you to finish your reports, but you can do that from home. I'd like you to take some time off. The doctor told me that Mary may be released in a day or two. We only asked because we want to make sure she doesn't cross paths with Yates as we are transporting him out of the hospital. The trial's going to already be a strain on her since it's almost a guarantee the prosecution will call her as a star witness. With her testimony alone, Yates will go away for the rest of his life. For now, the people that love her need to focus on helping her recover. So, take some vacation time and help her through this. You haven't taken a vacation in over two years, so I know you have the time, and you won't be far if I need something else."

The chief looked really uncomfortable, and Devon knew he was struggling to find the words to what he wanted to say next. "I really hope you know how sorry I am about how this all went down. This case made me realize that I'm overly ambitious. I was putting my ambitions before the safety of my agents and, in this case, above the safety of Ms. Anderson. I'm truly sorry, and it won't happen again. You're one of my best agents, and I hope you'll continue to serve under my leadership when this is all over."

Parker quickly turned and walked away before Devon had a chance to respond. That was the last thing he ever thought he'd hear his chief say, but he respected him even more for it. Just wait until he tells Matthews.

Devon quietly slipped back into Mary's room, not wanting to disturb her aunt and uncle. Moments later, the nurse came in and announced that visiting hours were over, and only one person could stay until visiting hours started again. Devon walked over to Mary's bedside, leaned down, and kissed her forehead. Before he could become emotional, he turned and moved towards the door when Mr. Carter stopped him.

"Agent Walker, thank you for everything you've done in not only finding our niece, but protecting her all these weeks. At first, I fought against someone other than my own people being responsible for Mary's safety, but I realized early on that I was wrong. You are the best thing that could've happened to our Mary. I'm not sure if you knew this, but she spoke of you often. She told us how much she was coming to admire you and care for you. We'll never be able to repay you, but if there's anything you ever need, all you need to do is ask. Now, we are going to leave and let you get some one-on-one time with our girl. Here is my card with my personal number. Please call me at any time, day or night, if there are any changes. Okay?"

Devon nodded. He would've thought Mary's uncle and his wife would refuse to leave her side, but he was thankful. Even if she was sleeping, he'd feel better just being close to her.

After they left, it was just him and Mary. What was he supposed to do now? He wanted to crawl into the bed, pull her into his arms, and never let go. The nurses might make a fuss if he did something like that. So instead, he took up the seat her aunt had occupied and reached out to take her hand. "I've got you, Mary. I'm sorry I couldn't protect you, but I'll make it my responsibility from this day forward to keep you safe, if you'll let me. We've only known each other a short time, but it feels like it has been years. You probably know me better than anyone else in my life. Just don't tell Matthews. He gets jealous. I love you, Mary. I've never told you that, but I do. It's true. I love you and I always will."

Devon leaned down and put his head on the bed. He knew he needed to rest, but he wouldn't leave her side. He fell asleep listening to the heart rate monitor that sounded like a beacon of hope. Throughout the rest of the night, he woke every time a nurse came into the room to check Mary and her machines.

After sunrise, he felt a little stirring under his hand. His head shot up and he saw Mary's eyes were open. She smiled, faint, weak and obligatory. "Good morning, beautiful."

Devon reached over and hit the nurse call button. He settled back down, reading the concern etched into her face. There was no hiding it behind even her bravest facade. "Oh, Mary, I'm so sorry." His voice broke as he spoke softly to her. "I'm so happy you're okay, and you're going to be okay, sweetheart. Nothing bad is ever going to happen to you again."

Tears sprang to Mary's eyes as tenderness and contentment raced through her.

A thought suddenly occurred to Devon that would make Mary very happy. Without letting go of her one hand, he reached behind him and retrieved his wallet from his back pants pocket and fumbled around. "I have something for you, love."

She wasn't able to see what he was doing, still too weak to pull herself up to look at her lap, but then she felt it. She felt the familiar weight on her finger and knew Devon had given her the most amazing gift. He gave back her mother's ring. She was devastated when Yates took it from her and never expected to see it again. Before she could attempt to tell Devon what this meant to her, they were interrupted.

The doctor was quick to come into her room and immediately noticed Mary was awake. "Mr. Walker, would you mind stepping out of the room while I give Ms. Anderson a quick examination?"

He hesitated only briefly. "Of course, Doctor. Mary, I'll be right outside. I'm going to call your aunt and uncle and tell them you're awake." He leaned down and gave her a quick kiss on the hand before walking out the door.

Her aunt and uncle made it to the hospital right as the psychologist finished talking to Mary. The psychologist quickly spoke to the doctor, and then the doctor came over to talk to them. "The psychologist's major concern right now is that Mary's not yet completely processed everything that's happened to her, and when she does, she'll likely experience symptoms of PTSD such as flashbacks and nightmares following such an extreme and traumatic event. PTSD is very common in victims of abuse and torture. We both spoke to Mary, and suggested she try not to talk unless it's absolutely necessary. The damage to her windpipe is extensive, but will heal with time. We both feel confident with therapy. She'll be able to work through what happened to her during her time in captivity. He's concerned with her being alone during this time. We have a list of inpatient facilities the social worker can provide."

Carter and his wife both turned to look at Devon, and Devon nodded. The congressman said, "no, we will have someone with her at all times." The doctor nodded and turned and walked away.

As soon as the doctor turned the corner, Mary's aunt gave Devon a quick hug, then rushed into her niece's room. She then threw her arms around Mary, engulfing her in a big hug, and cried again. Devon had never seen a person cry as much as Mary's aunt does, but in this case, she had justification to be as emotional as she wanted. Mary heard the door open again and lifted her head to look around at her aunt. A beautiful smile spread across her face the moment she saw Devon. All the pent-up worry that had been plaguing him went out the window with just that one smile. And he knew right then, Mary was going to be okay. She was hands down the strongest person he'd ever met. Who else could go through something like that and not have broken down or withdrawn into the darkness?

Her uncle moved to the side of the bed and leaned down and brushed his finger down Mary's cheek. "How are you feeling, sweetheart?" After what the doctor said, he didn't expect her to answer back, and that was okay. She reached over, grabbed his hand, and gave an affectionate squeeze. "How do you feel about going home? The doctors said we can take you home tonight and recommend someone stay with you for the next few weeks. You just need to tell us where you want to stay. Of course, you could come to stay with us, or one of us can stay with you at your home if you would prefer?" He gave a mischievous look at Devon, "Or I'm sure Devon has a spare room you can use for a few weeks." His wife reached over and smacked his arm.

Devon moved up to the side of the bed, looked down at Mary, and winked at her. "Yes, Sir. I'd be more than happy to have Mary stay with me at my place for a few weeks. It just so happens I was told to take a few weeks of vacation that I've been racking up."

Carter laughed, "Sir? Since when am I, Sir?"

Devon tried to suppress a smile. "Well, Sir. I figured if I'm going to try to convince your niece to be in a relationship with me, I need to show you the respect you deserve."

"Huh. Well, if my Mary will have you, you can call me Robert." He reached out his hand to Devon. As Devon shook his hand, Robert pulled him in so he could whisper in his ear. "Now, son, if I find out you hurt my Mary in any way, my security detail will make sure they never find your body. Is that understood?"

Devon didn't know whether to laugh or be genuinely frightened. He believed the congressman could make good on his threat. From what he saw of his security force, they'd do anything for him. Did he forget Devon was with the FBI? He doubted the congressman gave a damn about that. He only wanted what was best for his niece. "Completely understood, Robert. You don't have to worry about that. Now that I have Mary back, I won't let anything hurt her, even me."

"Mary," Robert said, turning to his niece, "would you want to spend some recovery time with Devon?"

Averting her eyes to her lap, Mary gave a simple nod, red spreading across her cheeks. Devon smiled. He loved that.

Then, suddenly, his phone buzzed from a text message. He was about to ignore it, but gave it a quick glance. It was a text from Chief Parker. Giving a slight head nod to Carter, "Robert, can I talk to you for a moment?"

Devon and Robert moved to the hall so Mary wouldn't hear what he had to say. "Chief Parker just sent me a message. They're getting ready to move Yates from this hospital to a supermax prison to recover. He needs me to go run interference while they get him out a different door to avoid the media. It's already a circus outside, and we don't need to give them any more fuel. It'll be bad enough in the coming weeks."

Robert rubbed his temples as if trying to ward off a headache. "Thanks for the heads up. I'll make sure Mary's curtains stay closed and her TV off. We don't need her catching a glimpse of that bastard and getting more upset. I won't leave her side until you get back."

Devon and Robert returned to Mary's room. Her aunt helped her into a sitting position, and Devon could see Mary was studying his face. She could tell something was going on that neither Devon nor her uncle wanted her to know about. Devon walked up and tenderly stroked her cheek. "I've got some work to do, then I'll be back. It shouldn't take me any longer than an hour. I know what you like to eat, and since I do all the cooking anyway, I'll take care of groceries."

Turning to Patricia, he asked, "Do you think you and Robert would be able to pick up what she needs from her apartment?" Patricia nodded, not taking her gaze off Mary's face.

Standing up, Devon moved towards the door. "I'll be back soon. Then we can talk to the doctor about springing you out of here. You'll be more comfortable at my home." Wanting to make sure she wasn't worrying about him, he leaned down and whispered in her ear. "Or, you could not have your aunt pick anything up and you can either wear my clothes or walk around naked." He heard an almost inaudible gasp, so he winked at her and turned to walk out the door.

Her aunt thought making a list was a wonderful idea, so she sprang to her feet to get a notepad and pen. Hopefully, it would keep Mary occupied while he was gone. Devon saw the look on her face before he left her room. She knew something was going on that they weren't telling her, but hopefully she'd let it go and not ask. Yeah, right. Mary was the smartest person he'd ever met. She'd figure out what was going on. Hopefully, it'd all be over before she had time to dwell on it.

Chapter 27

The secure wing Yates was being held on was an utter madhouse. Devon had to show his badge to two different hospital police officers before he could find a fellow FBI agent. "What's going on Scott?"

Agent Scott looked relieved to see Devon. "Dang, Walker, I'm glad you're here. It's a shit show for sure. The doctors are trying to get Yates out of the hospital as quickly as possible. The phones have been going non-stop with threats against Yates and even some threats against the hospital, unless they release him. One person even threatened to shoot their way through the hospital unless they released Yates to the public. We looked into it and it was unsubstantiated, but I guess the victims' family and friends want to take action into their own hands. Not that I blame them or anything. This guy is a monster. Do they really think the law wouldn't crucify him? He'll never breathe free air again."

"You have no idea the extent of his malevolence unless you read his old case files. I read through them when he first re-surfaced in D.C., and anyone that can do that to children was born from pure evil." Looking around the corridor, Devon couldn't spot Matthews or Chief Parker. "And, I can tell you, it's even worse to see in person."

Though Devon was busy searching for his partner, Agent Scott continued to talk. "I hear you. Just from the stories some of the MDP officers have been telling, Yates truly is a spawn of Satan. Oh! Hey, sorry, I forgot to ask, how's Mary doing?"

He turned back to Scott, "She's alive, and that's the most important part. She has a long road to recovery, but she is a fighter. Now, let's get this psycho out of this hospital before the people downstairs try making their way up here again."

"If you're looking for Chief Parker, he's down at the nurse's station across from the room Yates is being held in."

Devon turned and was just about to make his way toward his boss, when Parker and the nurse he was talking to suddenly rushed into Yates's room. A doctor called for security as they pushed through the door. Jimmy Yates was flailing on the bed with such force, blood was dripping from the handcuffs on his wrists. He locked eyes with Devon as he stepped into the room.

"You! This is all your fault. You couldn't just leave me and my business alone. Just another hour and the bitch would've been dead. Ahhh-hhh!" Yates screamed with venom in his voice.

How did he find out about Mary? Parker didn't want him told for this very reason. As amused as Devon was at Yates's pain, he wasn't going to stand there and listen to him say vile things about her. He smiled as he turned and walked out the door.

Parker was already back at the nurses' station demanding the doctor heavily sedate Yates for transport. Parker would call in the big guns if he doesn't get his way. If Devon was the doctor, he'd have given in by now. There's no winning against Parker, even if the doctors did swear some oath. Parker swore one too, and that trumped keeping him comfortable and awake.

Devon walked up next to Chief Parker as the doctor finally agreed to sedate Yates under the condition of safe transport because he was a danger to himself and others after receiving that news. This is the same doctor that, not long ago, Parker was berating for sedating Yates in the first place, and now he was ordering him to personally administer the drugs. Devon had to suppress a smile. The irony was too rich.

"Where do you need me, Chief?" Devon spoke up, catching the chief's attention. Until that moment, Parker was so absorbed with arguing with the doctor, he didn't realize Devon had walked up beside him.

"Oh, good, Walker, you're here. They're going to take Yates down the service elevator and to a white unmarked van that won't pull around the building until we're on our way out. We'll have two agents in the back with Yates, and one agent and one MPD officer in the front of the van. Once they pull out onto the public road, there'll be a police escort in the front and one in the back. Our vulnerable points are in transit, so once we move, we need to push on quickly and get him to the prison. I'm sure you already heard about the threats the hospital is receiving pertaining to Yates's safety and the general population's desire to dole out justice. With that mob of wannabe vigilantes outside, we need this to go as smoothly as possible.

"I want you stationed at the back of the hospital next to the service entrance. That's where the van will pull up. You just have to get the doors open on the van and on the building so it can be a quick, seamless transition. Head on down to your location and I'll send a text when we're on the move. It shouldn't be longer than twenty minutes. As soon as the meds kick in, we'll be moving. I want this over and done with, and Yates behind bars before the mob downstairs figures anything out."

It wasn't even fifteen minutes later when Devon received the text. It was go time. The media hasn't leaked information about the move, yet, so the crowd of people outside won't be checking for possible exits from the hospital. A leak was inevitable, though. Hopefully, it would come after Yates was secured inside the van. The last thing they needed was for some eager cameraman or a victim's family member running down the alley while they were trying to load Yates.

Checking again, Devon confirmed the back of the building was empty, and no pedestrian foot traffic. He heard the elevator open and saw the gurney being pushed in his direction. He looked back outside in time to see the unmarked white van make the turn. The van pulled to a stop as Parker guided the doctors, pushing Yates's gurney outside. Devon caught a flash coming off the neighboring building, and that's when all hell broke loose. In the blink of an eye, the world turned upside down.

"Get down," he yelled at the same time the first shot rang out. Three repetitive shots sounded before the agents could get back up. Parker was yelling into this radio for someone to get eyes on the shooter. Devon knew one shot hit the side of the van because he heard the ping not far from his head. He didn't realize until they pulled Yates back into the building exactly where the other shots hit. One-shot hit Yates in the neck, and the other in the chest. There was no doubt about it. He was dead. And with the heavy sedation, he didn't even suffer.

After everything that bastard had done to terrorize this country, he wouldn't get his time in court. Justice was not served today. Yates deserved to sit through a trial, knowing the verdict would end with a needle being inserted into his arm. Now, he'd never know the dread of watching the executioner loading the deadly liquid into the IV machine that would deliver death into his veins and stop his heart. No, that bastard deserved to suffer for what he'd done.

Everything was still a blur of motion inside the service entrance doors when another agent called Parker back within minutes, alerting him to the apprehension of the sniper. Yates killed the shooter's sister's entire family, and he was getting his form of revenge. To Devon, Yates got off too easy. He wanted Yates to sit in a jail cell, counting down the days until they stuck that needle in his arm. Devon would've been front and center in the witness room. He wanted to be the last thing Yates saw before he went to Hell. He wanted Yates to know that he'd lost and the law won. But now that would never happen. All of his victims had been robbed of justice.

Chapter 28

Even though they had the shooter in custody, the entire hospital was on lockdown. Devon had to flash his badge half a dozen times to get back to the floor Mary's room was on. Robert was waiting outside Mary's room when he walked up. "What the hell happened, Devon? Officers and doctors have been running around in a panic."

"Yates is dead. Someone got to him as we were moving him out of the hospital. Everyone was so worried about a ground attack, they didn't properly cover the rooftops." Devon shook his head in dismay. Damn, Parker was going to take some serious heat for that mistake. He may even lose his command for moving too quickly without proper preparation. "Anyway, it's over. Yates is dead. It's not the ending I would have wanted for him. I wanted him to suffer and know true terror before he died. At least now he can't hurt any more families, and the families of his victims can properly mourn."

Tears welled in Robert's eyes. "You're exactly right. I thought I wanted Yates to sit in prison for the rest of his life, but it's a relief to know he's no longer contaminating this earth with his existence. My sister- and brother-in-law and all his other victims never deserved to be murdered, and especially so young. It's not fair that they won't get to see the beautiful woman Mary grew up to be. Or meet their grandchildren and great-grandchildren. It's just not fair. At least a piece of each of them will live on with Mary, but now, hopefully, they can get some peace. Mary's safe now, and she'll always be loved. Patricia and I were never able to have children of our own, and in every way that matters, Mary is our daughter. We never would've imagined that to gain a child, we needed to lose my sister, Angela and her husband, Thomas.

"We've done our best, and hopefully, Angela is proud of us. I know they'd have loved you. My sister was just like Mary. She wore her heart on her sleeve." He wiped his eyes on his shirt. "Now, let's go in and distract Mary and Patricia. We have a few more hours before the doctor will release her, and I don't want her to find out what happened here today. She's not going to be forgetting anything that's happened to her anytime soon, and she'll find out eventually what happened, but not today."

They walked into the room to Mary laughing. It was the most beautiful sound, even though it was very muffled and raspy. Patricia was talking to Mary and Mary was writing something down for her on a piece of paper. Apparently, the doctor was right. When Mary tried to talk, it felt like razor blades in her throat. But at least she was interacting with people again. He wondered if she knew, on some level, that she didn't need to worry about Yates any longer? Well, Devon would make sure Mary didn't have to worry about anything in the future. If she'd let him, he'd never leave her side again. Devon had around two months to convince her to move in with him, rather than returning to her apartment. He could do it. He had faith in himself.

Mary's aunt and uncle left the hospital to go collect the items Mary would need for her stay with Devon. Mary then signed the discharge papers and dressed and sat on the side of the bed, waiting to leave. Devon had Matthews pull his car around to an employee entrance, so reporters didn't bombard her when they left.

By chance, one nurse let slip that Yates was killed, and for the first time since she woke, Mary felt free. After everything that man put her through, she knew at that moment it was really finally over. Yates wouldn't be able to take any more families away from their loved ones. He'd never be able to take the life of an innocent child ever again. His reign of torment was officially, and forever, over.

When the time came to leave, the nurse insisted Mary ride in a wheelchair to the car. Apparently, it was hospital policy. Devon was thankful Matthews could pick them up with not one photographer within sight. The trip to Devon's home was quiet, but peaceful. He reached over and held Mary's hand as he drove, and every once in a while, he'd feel her shiver.

"Mary, love, are you okay?" He quickly glanced in her direction. Mary had turned to face him, but didn't say anything, and nodded. "We'll be home soon, then you can relax."

She nodded again, and he brought his hand up to rest against her cheek.

Hours later, after settling into Devon's home, they finally got Mary's aunt to agree to go home for the night. She only agreed to leave because Mary wrote on her notepad that she was tired and was thinking of heading to bed. She was still covered head to toe in bandages, so a shower or bath was out of the question. Mary refused to have a home nurse, so her aunt offered to help her with a sponge bath and changed her dressings before carefully slipping into pajamas before helping her into bed.

Meanwhile, Devon and Robert were still discussing security in the living room. Devon was trying to assure him that his apartment was very safe and that he wouldn't let anything happen to Mary. Yates was gone, so the major threat was over, but now the craziness of the media attention was before them. Every news station in the country was covering the apprehension of Jimmy Yates. Robert wanted to take every precaution with his niece while she recovered.

Media outlets hadn't caught on that Mary was at Devon's apartment and not her own, but after a few days of being camped out there, they'd know something was off. With a little digging, they'd put the pieces together and figure out where she was staying. He'd give it a week before the media camped in his lobby, hoping to get a peek at Mary. Devon was one hundred percent confident, though. They'd never be able to make it past the extra security he hired. He didn't tell Mary about the added security officers because he didn't want her to worry.

Matthews already insisted on running any errands for them. He mentioned Mary promised he'd get a home cooked meal every time he delivered groceries. Devon had a feeling they'd be getting grocery deliveries almost every day, but that was okay. Without Matthew's help, they may never have found Mary in time. Devon told Robert they should be able to stay in the apartment for weeks without having to leave.

"Are you sure you shouldn't just take her away for a while until the media attention dies down? By next week, there'll be some other major scandal that will draw their attention somewhere else." Robert asked with worry in his voice.

Devon laughed and shook his head. "You know she has many more doctors' appointments she needs to be at in the coming weeks. I talked to the social worker and the doctors will make video appointment calls, and a nurse will come here to give her all her shots and new medications. So she won't need to leave the apartment. We can't just disappear. Trust me, no one will get to her while she's here with me. Okay?"

Reluctantly, Robert agreed. "If you change your mind, I'm sure I can find you guys a secluded beach house, or maybe even a private island." He slapped Devon's back as he walked towards the door.

After they left, Devon quietly made his way into Mary's room to check on her. She was laying down, but was still wide awake looking out the window into the night sky. He stood, leaning against the door-jamb, content to watch her. Almost four days ago, he didn't know if he'd ever see Mary again. Now she was back with him, and he never wanted to let her out of his sight.

He wasn't sure how long he was standing there, staring at her, when he finally noticed she was staring back. "Hey, I thought you were tired. Do you need me to get you anything to help you sleep? The doctor prescribed some sleeping medication."

She slowly lifted herself into a sitting position, grimacing with each movement. Devon rushed over to the bed and gently lifted her up and pushed pillows behind her back for support. "You just need to ask if you need help. Okay?"

Slightly nodding her head, she whispered, "I just don't want to be a bother. I hate feeling so weak."

He sat down next to her and pulled her into his arms. "It's okay to ask for help, especially after the hell you've been through. Use me, Mary. Anything you need."

"I do have something to ask if it is not too much trouble." Every word she spoke sounded so strained and full of pain.

229

"You can ask me anything. I'll do anything for you. I hope you know that."

"Will you stay with me tonight, and maybe just hold me? Every time I close my eyes, I see Yates and those damn rats. Once in the hospital, I could've sworn I felt them crawling on me. I just don't want to be alone."

He studied her face briefly. Sleeping next to her would not be a good idea with all the lustful thoughts running around in his head, but how could he tell her no? "Sure, let me go change and I'll be right back."

She watched him leave the room. She felt selfish asking him to stay with her, but she thought he needed it as much as she did. He put his life on the line searching for her, and the dark circles under his eyes indicated he hadn't slept much, or at all, since her kidnapping. Maybe having him next to her would allow both of them to get the rest they needed.

Devon came back into the room wearing an old FBI t-shirt and mesh shorts. He looked exhausted. He lifted the blankets and crawled into bed. Removing the pillows from behind Mary, he pulled her down into the crook of his arm. She rested her head on his shoulder and let out a sigh, closing her eyes. She focused on Devon's breathing, and it calmed her.

Mary woke the next afternoon feeling refreshed. Thinking she'd go right to sleep last night was a mistake. They ended up staying awake most of the night, talking. That time spent in the dark was like nothing she's ever experienced. After spending a month cooped up in her apartment with Devon, she figured she knew him pretty well, but she didn't even scratch the surface until last night.

They started off talking about Yates and what happened to her. Devon thought it would help her to talk about it, and he helped her accept it was over. Yates would never be able to touch her again. After a few hours, they gradually drifted into talking about memories and dreams for the future.

Devon was content holding her in his arms, watching her sleep, but her fitfulness didn't escape his notice. In the wee morning hours, after Mary was able to fall asleep, she had haunting dreams. Devon stayed up all night holding her in case she needed him.

"You know, I've never spent the night with a woman without sex," Devon said. He was trying to keep a straight face, but when Mary looked up at him with scrunched brows and a gaping mouth, he burst out laughing. He pulled her closer. His lips brushed her temple. "Oh Mary, you're one extraordinary woman. With everything you've been through in your life, you are still so full of joy and light and complexity."

She lightly giggled, then coughed with pain. "Should I take that as a compliment?" She rasped.

"You absolutely should take that as a compliment, and only the highest one because it's the truth." His arms tightened around her again. "Do you realize how rare of a woman you are? After the experiences you've been through, to put it mildly, most people would be struggling."

"Stop analyzing me, Devon. You're the reason I'm handling this as well as I am. I honestly don't know where I'd be without you. You've been with me every step of the way. You brought me out of this, and right now, you're my rock. I'm not sure where this thing between us is heading, but I hope it continues."

He reached over and brushed a strand of hair behind her ear. "I feel that I've been heading in that direction since I stepped foot into your classroom, so I have a bit of a head start on you. If I'm lucky, maybe you'll meet me halfway?"

She was already more than halfway; Mary thought. She'd never felt as close to anyone as she did to Devon right now. But tragedy seemed to follow her wherever she went. Maybe she should distance herself in case he decides to one day leave her. "We're completely different. Maybe this isn't so sensible. Do you think we're feeling this way because we were both in an overemotional state of ...?"

"Shh." His fingers touched her lips, instantly silencing her. "Stop over-analyzing everything, love. Just give into whatever you are feeling, Mary. Give into this happiness and let it overwhelm you with joy. With your permission, I would love to see where this takes us. I think it'll be somewhere very special."

"Devon, I know what you're saying, but it is like a black cloud follows me w–" she argued, but he stopped her again.

"Mary, you don't fight these feelings. You no longer have anything to fear. You are free to live your life and love with your whole heart. Trust those emotions. I have a feeling it will lead us to incredible places." He nudged her chin up and leaned down. Kissing her gently, he whispered, "together, love."

Tears streamed down her cheeks. "Yes, Devon, together."

Epilogue

The glass barely made a crunch as it slammed into the wall next to the TV. Sitting in the living room, in a haze of cigarette smoke, destroying a glass wasn't enough. As the evening news came on the TV, the story of the capture and murder of the infamous serial killer, Jimmy Yates, dominated every station. How could he allow himself to get caught? No, it was obvious how it happened. It was his obsession with that bitch, Mary Anderson.

Mary'd been the only regret Yates had ever had in his amazing career. There was a time when it seemed he'd finally let go of his failure, took someone under his wing and taught the finer skills he would need to build a legacy no one would soon forget, but it seemed he couldn't let go after all. He couldn't get Mary out of his head. In the last few months, he was getting sloppy. He chose families with a daughter resembling the girl that got away. He was moving away from his rules, and it proved to be his downfall.

Now that Yates was gone, he wasn't the one picking targets anymore. What a perfect time to do one last job to honor the fallen mentor before leaving the stifling confines of D.C. That'd make Yates proud, finally. He was always saying awful things like 'you're a terrible student' and 'you'll never learn at this rate', as if it helped. Well, no more. Now, the student would become the master and do what the teacher never could.

"Watch out Mary, I'm coming for you."

Acknowledgments

I owe every thanks to my team at Flick-It-Books Publishing. My publisher, Misti, who supported both me and my novel during a time of uncertainty in my writing career. There are no amount of words that could express my gratitude for the support you've shown me. I also owe much to my editor, Glysia, who pushed me to take my writing to the next level. She took me out of my comfort zone, which I found is an amazing place to be. A big thank you to Cassie, my cover designer from Booklytical Designs. You turned my vision for my book cover into something I never could've imagined it becoming. You are a true artist. And finally, I'm eternally gratefully for all the love and support I've received from my husband and daughters over the past two years that I've spent brining this book to life. Thank you, everyone!!

Nicole Keefer is a writer whose military experience and educational background in criminology and forensic psychology provide her with the vast inspiration and insight she needs to create riveting characters. Writing a novel was always on her bucket list, and eventually, with MY SAVIOR, it became a reality. When not reading or writing, Nicole enjoys spending time with her family. Nicole lives in Michigan with her husband and daughters. HIS VICTIM'S TOMRENT is book one of her first serial killer duology.

CPSIA information can be obtained
at www.ICGtesting.com
Printed in the USA
BVHW040347050523
663630BV00001B/5